MAKERSEX

MAKERSEX

EROTIC STORIES OF GEEKS, HACKERS, AND DIY CULTURE

EDITED BY ANNABETH LEONG

CIRCLET PRESS, INC.
CAMBRIDGE, MA

MakerSex: Erotic Stories of Geeks, Hackers, and DIY Culture
edited by Annabeth Leong

Printed in the United States.
ISBN: 978-1-61390-159-5

Print-on-demand edition.

For catalog, information about our imprints, review copies, and other information, please write to:

Published by:
Circlet Press, Inc.
39 Hurlbut Street
Cambridge, MA 02138

Or visit us online at: http://www.circlet.com

CONTENTS

INTRODUCTION

"I don't like this hotel," he said. "We should do something about that."

He was an insomniac who listened to Danzig while doing pushups in the middle of the night and plotting his eventual glorious hacker coup. I had spent the last several years wringing every bit of computer knowledge I could from him. Not having access to the Internet at my place, it was the only way I knew to learn new commands for DOS Shell.

Around him, I tended to get into adoring listening mode. So, while I am not normally given to revenge or pranks, I nodded my agreement. "Yeah, we should."

"We should rewire the telephone in this room."

I blinked. "How would we do that?"

"We'd need a soldering iron."

"Oh. That makes sense." I wasn't really sure what a soldering iron did, but it seemed right that an undertaking such as rewiring a telephone would require special equipment. "I guess we can't, then."

He shrugged. "I've got one in my bag."

Another blink. "You travel with a soldering iron?"

"We need one now, don't we?"

We unplugged the telephone from the wall and carried it into the bathroom. As fascinated as I was with him, it's the telephone I remember.

It revealed its secrets as we opened it up (using a screwdriver he also carried in his bag). I couldn't have interpreted every wire and circuit board, but soon I could see the basic shape of how we would accomplish the plan. He wanted to change the phone so it registered a different number than intended when you pushed a button. It wasn't hard to guess which wires we needed to move.

Soon, the harsh scent of solder stung the back of my nose as we used little globules of it to reattach the wires we had changed.

As I write this now, it's hard to understand what we thought we were accomplishing. At most, we caused some later guest a few moments of confusion, and that was neither nice nor logical.

On the other hand, I have few memories that are so vivid. I felt grand in that moment, soldering iron cradled in an awkward but reverent grip. The ground shifted beneath me. I thought love was doing that to me, but really it was wonder. I had discovered that a telephone had an inside and that I could change it.

For years, my partner and I had been fantasizing about chair dildos. We loved the idea of me sinking down on one and then trying to do something ordinary, like eat breakfast. We were very into the dissonance between what would be going on above the kitchen table and what we would know was happening below the table.

The fantasy was so good and so inspiring to us that I was afraid to make it real. Toys had disappointed us before. Finally, I couldn't resist anymore. I obtained the necessary components and set up the chair dildo for us to enjoy.

It was everything we'd dreamed it could be, possibly hotter in real life than it had been in the fantasy. I finished breakfast with a shattering orgasm.

I noticed a funny thing at that point, though. I felt sated, complete, and happy. I didn't want or need to do anything else. However, I felt bad because that wasn't how an erotic story was supposed to go. I knew the formula well, especially as an erotica writer: we were supposed to try this cool, sexy experiment, and then maybe I could have an orgasm during the foreplay this experiment allowed, but then I was supposed to take my partner to the bedroom and "actually" fuck.

For all that I believed in sexual creativity, I wasn't as open-minded about sex as I thought. I still had a lot of ideas about what did and didn't count as sex, what I was supposed to do to be a good sexual partner, and what sex was supposed to look like. I asked my partner about this, and we both agreed we were satisfied by the enactment of this super-great chair dildo masturbation fantasy. Since then, I have consciously tried to open sex up and look inside, to see what components it contains, and to decide whether I want to change them. Because now I know I can.

I grew up with the idea that things bought off the shelf were somehow safer or more proper. "Can't we just buy one?" I would ask whenever I wanted to be sure something worked just right. Jam canned at home might have some weird bacteria in it. A video game with a mod installed would probably run buggy. Sex that didn't involve certain specific acts was probably not really sex at all, but rather something lesser and less important.

It took a long time for me to see that these ideas are connected. The power I felt from looking inside a telephone and realizing I could change it is something like the power I felt from thinking about what I actually wanted to do with the new chair dildo and realizing I could stop whenever I felt satisfied.

In a lot of ways, I got the message that I shouldn't tamper with things, shouldn't void the warranty, shouldn't act weird. Maker culture is sending a more interesting message. It's about figuring how to make or alter things so they work for you, in ways that appeal to you. Maybe those projects are world-changing, or maybe they're just neat. Either way, they're powerful because they're about taking ownership, seeing the insides of things, and realizing that you can affect the way they work.

When I put out a call for stories about Makers, it was partly because I've always found skill sexy. Tell me that you know how to weld, or that you have a basket full of projects involving conductive thread, or that you've used R to code up your own quirky analysis of your favorite TV show, and you'll have, at the very least, my undivided attention.

It was also because I've always found rebels sexy. In my

experience, once you learn to look inside things, it's easy to start thinking differently. It's no accident that Maker culture is full of rebels and punks.

Most of all, what I wanted were stories that hit all these notes. I wanted curious rebels overflowing with skill and artistry. I wanted to see projects that inspired characters to seek their own pleasure in the form they wanted it to take, not just suffer through the sex they'd been told they ought to enjoy. I wanted fascination and wonder—and a shattering orgasm or six.

The stories I received delivered. These authors have created worlds I never want to leave, projects that make me want to pull out the soldering iron right now, and sexual connections that leave me breathless. I hope you enjoy these views of the insides of things, and that they inspire you to many projects (and orgasms) of your own.

—Annabeth Leong
Providence, Rhode Island
March 2016

THE NOT SO WHOLESOME ORIGINS OF CUDDLE-BOT

LILLIAN MARGUERITE

Layla put down her soldering iron as Jason walked to the door. As he got nearer to it, she leaned, following him with her body until she nearly toppled out of her chair. She hopped up as the door closed behind him. "We have to do something for Jason," she said, addressing the other two left in the space.

Khaled sat in a beanbag chair near the bookshelf, his laptop balanced on his broad knees, his soft features thoughtful as usual. "Is it his birthday?"

Tall, lean Derek stood by the loading-dock doors, holding a chain he was threading through the gears on his latest kinetic sculpture. "He in trouble?"

Layla groaned melodramatically. She opened the front door and looked up and down West Baltimore Avenue. Downtown Detroit was quiet on a Sunday morning, the sunrise still painting the parking garage opposite their little storefront hackerspace. She closed the door and locked it. "You know how Jason doesn't like to be touched?"

"Tell me this isn't an intervention," Derek said. "Live and let live."

"No! It's nothing like that." She walked to the center of the room and waved the guys toward her. After some hesitation, and looking at each other as if for support, Khal set his laptop down and Derek lowered his chain. They joined her in front of the circuit board assembly bench where she'd been working. She put a hand on each man's shoulder. "Here's the scoop. I was talking with Jason last night, when we were the last two here, and he told me—he does want romantic companionship."

"That's good," Khal said. His muscular arm was warm and thick, wrapping around her shoulders. "You know, I just love Jason to death."

"Tell me this isn't a hook up," Derek said.

"Sort of." Layla bit her lip. "Honestly, I think he's sad, and the only thing to do, as his friends, is build him a cuddle-bot."

Derek raised an eyebrow. "Cuddle-bot?" He rested the small of his back on the edge of Layla's bench. He had that way of looking comfortable in impossible positions, like a cat.

"Jason explained it to me—he doesn't like the warmth and sweat of skin. He wants to be touched, but not by living things."

"It could work," Khal said. "We'll need excellent pressure sensors and a tunable tolerance algorithm so it doesn't hug too hard or too light."

Derek shook his head again. "There are stores where we can buy the boy a sex doll."

"Cuddle-bot," Layla said. "And it should be custom, don't you think? Not human-like. Of course, if you're not up to the challenge of designing hugging arms...."

"Oh, you did not." Derek straightened.

Layla batted her eyelashes.

"We'll need it to detect preference," Khal said. He broke away from the group. "Pheromone receptors! Maybe facial mood recognition?" He went to the whiteboard and started a list, drawing boxes labeled "software" and "hardware."

"I'll do the electronics," Layla said. "Khal will write the software. You can make the body. We're the perfect team."

Derek bit his lip. He watched Layla and Khal talking excitedly by the whiteboard. Layla erased something Khal had written with her small, round hand and wrote something in its place, and they both chimed, "Of course!" Layla was dark and plump with a cute face and full breasts. Khal was thick with muscle, his lighter skin stretched yellow against the strain of his biceps.

Derek looked at his abandoned sculpture, and then at the 3D printer. They had some materials he'd been dying to play with. Jason was a student at Wayne State, a chemical engineer, and had introduced some damn sexy new mixes. Derek loved Jason, and he was getting hot watching Layla and Khal work. He sighed and walked up between his friends, arms crossed. "Let's talk about the joints. Can we create a ball joint control with four friction wheels?"

Layla squeezed his waist. "I knew you'd help."

"Well, I'm not going to let you two have all the fun."

"This is a lover." Derek held the prototype hand against his chest. Long, articulated fingers splayed against his muscle, seeming to stroke him as he moved them down. "You can't make it sensitive *enough*."

Khal gestured impatiently at the whiteboard. "But the more controls there are, the higher the processing burden."

Layla danced over with a soldering iron in one hand and a circuit board in the other. She kissed Khal's cheek. "I got you more processing power. Come see."

Khal frowned. "I don't need to see. Just send me the specs."

Layla pouted but went back to her workbench. "You know what I love about Jason? He gets excited about everyone's projects, not just his own."

Derek dropped the prototype hand against Khal's broad chest. "This is your problem, man. You're so uptight. You're not enjoying the process."

Khal hunched protectively over his laptop, holding his hands out, and exposing delicious ripples of flesh from the sides of his XKCD muscle shirt. "I'm building an elaborate, invisible chandelier—all bulbs at once. I'll relax when the center post is done."

"Programmers," Derek muttered. "I'm making *art* here." Derek was a student at the College for Creative Studies, which was just down the road. He secretly worried that Khal, with his cushy job writing software for GM, didn't respect his work.

"This processing unit is art," Layla said, looking down at her work, her face hidden by her magnification goggles. "It's sexy as *fuck* too."

"Maybe it's time to start talking about other functions," Derek said. He brushed his hip against Khal and let the disembodied hand stroke down his own abdomen.

"You...." Khal glanced at the pale plastic fingers cupping Derek's groin and looked away again, a blush lighting up his dusky cheeks. "You're off mission."

"Blame Layla for saying 'sexy as fuck.'"

"That's all it takes?" Khal sounded disgusted, but he snuck another look at Derek through his lowered lashes.

Derek shrugged. He affixed the arm to the body he was assembling on a sculpture stand. He had to crouch—they were building the robot to Jason's height, and he was a good head shorter than Derek. He swayed a bit, as though dancing to a silent soundtrack, something slow and sultry, while he worked. "This. Bot. Is. Sexy. You have to feel this silicone composite. It is the sexiest plastic you'll ever kiss."

"I don't kiss plastic," Khal said.

"I do." Layla set her soldering iron in its holder and came over. She stroked the smooth, ovoid chest of the cuddle-bot. "Wow. That is sexy. It's like... not like skin... like silk."

"This is tactile porn. Jason made it." Derek embraced the half-completed torso and slow danced with it. He imagined his touch transferring to Jason through the silicone, showing him how he cared. Layla crowded up behind him, her hands on his hips.

"You guys," Khal said, blushing and stealing glances as he pretended to concentrate on his work. Layla and Derek were studies in contrast—her curves busting out of her clothes while he was long and lean. Khal could hear the brush of denim on denim and smell the commingled sweat of his two friends.

"You're getting me too hot. Go finish the spine wiring." Derek kissed Layla on the cheek and unbuttoned his shirt.

Derek threw his shirt in a corner and picked up the next arm to attach. Khal wondered what that washboard stomach would feel like under his hands.

Layla stroked the completed arm. "I'm going to give this baby so much power."

"Seriously," Derek said. "Go. Or I won't get the rest assembled."

Layla gave his butt a hard squeeze and sauntered over to Khal's area. Khal quickly refocused his attention on his screen.

"We really need more features," Layla said. Her breasts pressed against Khal's back as she looked over his shoulder.

Khal shifted. "You're hot."

"Thanks. So I've been told." Her hand lingered on his chest.

Derek dragged the bot to the center of the room. "Voila! Arms and legs."

The smooth torso tapered down to a ball-like hip. Three arms hung from the top, and three legs from the bottom. The arms rested in upward Vs; the legs flexed on shock-absorbing knees.

Layla sauntered up to it. "Wait... you can add more balance sensors if I add a line going here." She let her fingers linger between two metal legs. Then Layla hurried to her bench. The bot's circuitry lay in a loose tangle. "You know, I'm not working tomorrow. We can go all night at this."

"Oh, I can go all night," Derek agreed.

Khaled exhaled quickly. He really had to start concentrating on this code!

Temporarily done with his part, Derek watched Layla work. Her small hands were quick and sure. She was the only one of them not to have gone to college, but he didn't doubt she had a brilliant future ahead of her once the world took notice of her skill.

While she tucked the wires into the limbs, Derek rummaged around the bins of old parts. "Hey, what do you think about this?"

He held up a dildo.

"We don't really know what Jason is into," Layla said.

"All the more reason to prepare for all options." Derek waved it. "I think maybe I can find something inflatable—simulate tumescence with contact?"

Her juicy lips formed a soft circle. "Oo, I like!"

Derek picked up another object. "I took the liberty of taking apart a Fleshlight. We had one in the donated electronics bin, believe it or not. Now, look how these ball bearings move when I turn on the motor."

Khal sunk lower behind his laptop. Layla brushed his hair back from his sweaty forehead. "Is this bothering you, Khal?"

"No, I'm fine," he said, in a higher-pitched voice than he usually had.

"You sure about that, hon?"

His laptop slipped from his hands and onto the chair beside him. Derek smirked. Normally Khal treated his laptop like his baby, but he didn't even look at it.

Layla leaned over his shoulder, her eyes exaggeratedly flicking up and down, drawing Derek's attention to the very visible tent in Khaled's jeans. "Oh," she said. "Is that it?"

Khal shifted anxiously. "I... you keep talking about...."

"Khal? Sweetie, I think we've all been turned on for about an hour. It's okay."

"I don't want you to think...."

Layla dropped her hand into Khaled's lap and gave his shaft a gentle squeeze through the tough denim. She leaned close so she felt just a brush of his ear against her lips. "Want me to think what?"

Khal squeaked.

Derek sat down next to the beanbag. "So I guess I could show you this Fleshlight idea more up-close, huh?"

With a grunt, Derek finished pulling the silicone rubber sleeve over its new housing. The Fleshlight was a masturbation tool shaped like a tube with molded lips on one end—a tight channel for the owner to work over a penis. Derek had replaced the interior silicone with ball bearings on a spiral track. He closed the power contact, and the fake lips pursed and twisted with the motion of the throat behind them and the steady whine of the ball bearings sliding under the skin. He held the housing out to Khal. "Stick your finger in that. Feel it."

Khal did so while Layla undid his jeans. Khal's eyes widened. "It... it feels like it's pulling... sucking." The boys both had their mouths open, close enough that they had to be breathing in each other's exhales.

"Nice trick of pressure, huh? You want to try it, Layla?"

Layla didn't want to distract them from each other. "Oh, I've got something to pressure right here, thanks."

"I don't... I don't know if... we'll need a... sensor... if something is inserted." Khal slid off the beanbag, his legs opening wider as Layla worked his cock out of his underwear. "I wouldn't want to... interrupt the smooth inner... oh god... surface."

"That's easy," Layla said. "Put the sensor behind the fake skin, make it sensitive enough to detect insertion through it."

"We could do that," Derek said. "But I think we should test that it works, first."

Layla obligingly held Khaled's dick, massaging it gently while Derek pushed the former Fleshlight down over the head. "Tell us everything you're experiencing, Khal. This is for science."

"*Oh god.*"

"Hrm." Derek nodded thoughtfully. "I'll take that as a successful test.

Layla knelt between Khal's legs. She pressed her groin against the metal housing of the Fleshlight. "It's not doing much for me."

"Maybe I can help with that, too," Derek said. He straddled Khal's left leg and nibbled Layla's neck. He slipped one hand into her panties while his other pulled her hip back, flush against his hard-on.

Layla let go of the Fleshlight to wriggle out of her jeans. Khaled cried out as it fell over, picking it up himself at the last minute and settling back into the rhythm Layla had established. He looked embarrassed.

Layla kissed him and felt clever fingers inching her top up. Derek unclasped her bra, then his hands slid down, brushing along the top of her jeans and then down between denim and flesh in the front. Layla helpfully lowered her zip while Derek's fingertips pressed her damp panties into her.

She pulled the Fleshlight off Khaled and threw it over her shoulder. "I don't think I can stand much more of this foreplay."

Derek helped get the jeans out of the way, then he nibbled along her shoulder and rubbed his dick against her ass while she impaled herself on Khaled. She sighed in contentment. "That's better."

Khal reached past her, grabbing Derek's slender hips and pulling them both flush. Layla gasped her approval.

Derek watched Khal lick Layla's plump little nipples.

"I think one of us isn't having as much fun," Derek said. He pulled back and shucked his jeans. "I think I'm going to need the lube."

Layla leaned back, her fingers grasping for him. He obliged by stepping close. Her hair felt wonderful brushing across his heated flesh. She drove him with her hands on his hips, guiding him to her side. She gave his exposed cock a long lick and swallowed the tip. He gasped and flexed forward. She pulled off with a sucking pop. "Khal, sweetie, taste this. It's delicious."

She ran her thumb along Khal's lower lip, and he obligingly sucked her digit in and let her guide him to the head of Derek's cock.

Derek felt Khal's throat opening and gasped. "You sneak. You've done this before." Khal shook his head, but managed to look smug with a mouth full of cock.

Derek felt Layla's body moving up and down against him, her hot breath on his hip as she watched. "I'm not going to last," he said.

Layla pushed on Khal's chest. He pulled off Derek with an obscene pop. Layla said, "Lube. In my drawer, under the workbench."

As Derek crossed the room as quickly as he could, Khaled showed himself to be not so shy anymore. He lifted Layla and flipped her over. She laughed as her hands slapped the floor, and pushed her hips back against him.

Derek's mouth was dry from how gorgeous the two of them looked, writhing and fighting against each other in a battle to get off first.

He fumbled open the desk drawer and didn't have any trouble picking out the giant white tube of KY from among the diodes and electrodes. He wisely decided not to ask why she kept that there.

Derek squeezed a generous amount of lube onto his aching cock and rubbed it in as he walked back to them. He dropped down behind Khal and stroked his back, waiting for some sign of objection or shyness. Khal just grunted. His ass was flexing with his powerful thrusts into Layla, who, if her gasps and groans were anything to go by, was having an excellent time. Still, Derek made himself move slow, slipping just one finger down Khal's crack, finding his hole and circling it gently without entering. He squeezed more lube onto his fingers and repeated, and Khal pushed back, impaling himself.

Insertion resistance! He needed to check on the elasticity of the materials on hand, perhaps build an elastic structure into the bot's orifices.

"Hurry up," Khal said, with sudden impatience. "I'm not going to last."

Derek shuddered. He lubed up two fingers and pushed them in, scissoring frantically to loosen the muscle. Khaled slowed his thrusts to accommodate.

"I don't want to hurt you," Derek said.

"You'd better not hurt him," Layla shouted, "I don't want this dick going soft!"

Khal lay down over Layla, covering her with his body, lifting his ass to Derek's ministrations. Derek had three fingers in him now, and moved them in surer strokes. He decided that was enough and lined himself up.

Khal cried out as Derek slid home. Derek steadied him with a gentle hand. Khal was almost too tight, but then he bore down, muscles opening, welcoming Derek. Derek's eyes slid back in his head, and he held still to relish the sensation. Layla pushed back, urging them back into motion. For a moment they were all fighting each other, slipping out, failing to line up, but quickly they established a rhythm and became like a perfect set of pistons in line, working together in mechanical harmony.

Derek ran his hands over Khal and Layla, loving the difference in the texture of their skins and the union, the synchronicity of hip in front of hip. He reached under to touch Layla's clit and felt Khaled's fingers already there. Their fingers entwined together, and he felt Khal's dick driving into her soft folds behind them. It was hot and filthy and sweaty and Derek found himself already on the edge.

Cuddle-bot needed... pistons... and folds... and sweet, filthy smiles and broad shoulders and plump hips... new design ideas flooded over Derek.

Layla screamed first, stiffening. Her hips slammed back hard and she lifted against them with surprising strength, as though to milk the last moment of climax from them. Khal must have tipped over the edge from that, because his body clenched around Derek and he howled. It was a chain reaction. Derek's vision whited out, and he felt his body explode.

They fell into a sticky, satiated heap at the base of their semi-completed robot.

Layla rolled over and flicked sweat-damp hair from her eyes. She looked up at the robot. "Derek, see if you can get a cock on that thing. I want to test it out."

Derek stumbled off the bean bag chair, which he hadn't even realized he was kneeling on, and laughed as his legs failed to take his weight. He staggered to pick up the discarded Fleshlight.

"You're ready to go again?"

She fluttered her eyelashes. "It would be wrong to turn the product over without thorough testing."

Khaled watched Derek crawl all over the bot, testing each insertion point with finger, tongue and cock. He moved like a contortionist while Layla rocked against the bot's midsection. Derek and Layla designed a phallus together and printed it in the same soft silicone as the machine's body. It was designed to inflate, and could tuck behind a smooth door when not in use.

"Let's make... unh... sure it can take all the thrusting we can give it!" Layla said, and Derek crawled behind her. The two of them rocked hard and fast, and the bot gave as good as it got, without so much as a squeak.

Khaled was thinking about his load-distribution code when he noticed Layla staring at him. She gave him a saucy wink, and then her big lashes flicked toward Derek.

Khal set down his sports drink and stood, surprised to find he was hard again. He sauntered up behind Derek and stroked Layla's sweat-glistening side. "We should test the software as well as the hardware," he said.

Derek grunted, "There's... nothing... soft... here."

"Well," Khal said, swaying his hips to feel the light, teasing pressure on his cock as it grew even harder, "We'll just have to test to failure, then."

They were very vigorous in their testing, and Cuddle-bot did not fail.

It was a good thing Derek made three arms.

Jason came into the hackerspace the next morning to find his friends all frantically retrieving bits of clothing from every available surface.

"Ta da!" Layla said, still struggling to pull her bra strap over her shoulder while she waved at the strange-looking robot in the center of the space. It was very shiny: wet, like it had just been washed.

"Uh, Jason, meet Cuddle-bot," Derek said. He had a towel in his hands. He flicked it toward the body. "Cuddle-bot, Jason."

"It's a present. For you," Layla said.

"To cuddle," Khaled said, and then, inexplicably, blushed.

Jason walked around the robot. It was clear how it was intended to be used. There were arms, and a torso, all pleasantly clean and rounded and not sticky or sweaty or organic. "That's... thank you." He looked at Layla. "I assume this was your idea."

"Well, the boys did as much work on it as I did, design-wise."

"Hold still. I'm going to hug you, and I don't want you to move while I do it."

"Okay." Layla held still, smiling while Jason briefly clasped her and then stepped back.

He wasn't sure what all the extra plates and sensors on the bot were for, and he assumed they were unnecessary features. When he brought it home that night, he set it down next to his chair and it gave him a wonderful hug.

MAKING LOVE
RENATA PIPER

Auska stormed in with tears on her face. She threw herself down onto Iri, who waited just a moment—gauging body temperature, muscle tension, and the tempo at which Auska shivered—before wrapping her in both arms. "It's all right," Iri whispered. "All right, my dearest. I've got you. You're okay."

A full second later, Auska shrieked and kicked out hard. This was typical, and Iri had already made a soft space to allow for it, with enough resistance to make it satisfying and not enough to damage either of them. Iri held on with firm, steady pressure, until Auska had wept her way to exhaustion. Then Iri moved her, arms still around Auska's shoulders and waist, so that she was lying comfortably on her back with her head and feet propped up. Iri produced a silk handkerchief, which Auska dutifully used, and sent down to the kitchen for a cup of hot milk with honey. "He doesn't love me." Auska sniffled, burying her face in the silk.

The kitchen cart rolled up and chimed, settling down beside them to keep the drink warm. Iri considered saying several things, then decided on, "No, probably not. He hardly knows you. He's handsome and insecure, and you were exotic to him. Do you love him?"

Auska muttered, deliberately incomprehensible, then put aside the handkerchief and drank some milk. Her dark hair clung to her damp cheeks, and she swiped it aside. "Probably not," she said, adding savagely, "I wanted him to." Iri hummed and Auska leaned back, sprawling as she did, knees apart and arms out, the soles of her feet clamped together. Iri thumped Auska's street-stained boots, and Auska whispered an apology and took them off. Her toes clenched and unclenched, and she finished her drink, but she did not fall asleep. She spent a while humming, drumming her heels against Iri's side. Without being asked, Iri turned on a certain light, and Auska squinted into it, watching the patterns it made through her long eyelashes. Then Auska's younger brother called up that it was time for dinner, and Auska yelled back, *Coming!* and got up and went. The kitchen cart followed her, taking the empty cup.

Iri settled back into a more usual shape, a small curved sofa, sleekly upholstered and faintly avant-garde with layered arms. A little housekeeping bot rolled up, collected the boots and the handkerchief, and took them off to the laundry. The sun was setting outside the room's wide windows, burning rainbow-gold across Iri's iridescent surfaces and making the rest of the furnishings—kneeling desk, hanging swing, wardrobe, bookshelves, mattress-corner with its curtains and piles of pillows—gleam in their walnut and white. Auska's drawings and calligraphy, oversized and stately, stood out against the deep-green walls; between them were her degrees and certifications with their Latin inscriptions and baroque golden frames. Everything was as it should be, but Iri was uneasy. They had often spoken about love before, and sometimes Auska cried. But it had generally been theoretical, and practical problems were always worse. It bothered Iri that Auska should feel unloved.

It was very late when Auska returned, with grass-stains on her clothes and leaves in her hair. "Finn jumped me from the apple tree," she said, laughing, "and Ebba pulled him down from behind, and we made him bite a green apple before we let him up." Iri laughed back; Auska's siblings were all right, even when they fought. Auska disappeared into the bathroom, then came out naked with steam rising from her hair. "Iri," she said, "could you make love to me please?"

It was the phrasing that threw Iri—Auska usually said *get me off*—but the hesitation was just too long. "Of course," Iri said, but Auska was shaking her head already, hurrying to her corner of pillows and silk blankets.

"Never mind," said Auska. "Of course you can't. I'll get myself off, never mind."

"What do you mean I can't?" asked Iri, listening as Auska rummaged for a toy, wrapped herself tight in a blanket.

"Because you can't feel it," said Auska patiently. "Don't say it,

I mean, I know you feel it, I know you like to do it. But you can't feel it like sex, like love. You're a sofa."

"I am not a piece of furniture," said Iri icily. "I am an artificially intelligent individual, no more soulless than your wetware self." That part of the argument was old; they had settled it between themselves years before.

"You don't have sex parts, though," said Auska reasonably, sitting back up in bed. The blanket fell from her shoulders, revealing her breasts, and Iri wondered if that were true. But seeing Auska's bared body with a love-bite (not love, Iri remembered, so just a bite) still showing from that young man, and wishing that *of course I'll make love to you* had come out a moment sooner, Iri disagreed.

"I have parts enough to get you off," said Iri tartly. "You saw to that when you were twelve." Which was true. It was still the largest set of modifications they had ever made to Iri's structure. The ensuing reupholstery had already been overdue by virtue of childish wear and tear, and Auska's early habit of plucking at any loose threads. But Iri's collection of sensuous supplies and the dexterity to wield them had been a triumph of mutual experimentation and engineering, and it hurt to have it dismissed.

"That's not what I mean," said Auska, a little sadly, wrapping her arms around herself. "Iri, you know I love you. But when I can't do the same kind of thing for you, it can't be the same." Her fingertips dug hard into her own biceps. Not for the first time, Iri wished to go to her, to lift her into a tight embrace. But they had agreed, first at the behest of Auska's parents and later, more reluctantly, between themselves: Iri could be Auska's friend and resource, but should not try to be her savior. So Iri waited, arms held very still. "I'd want," said Auska, and stopped.

"Want what?"

"For you to feel like I do," said Auska in a rush. "Like your heart is exploding. Like your vision's gone all stars. Like we're melting together through our skins... Iri. You don't even masturbate."

That was true, but Iri caught hold of one of Auska's earlier phrases. "We could do the vision." There was a long, breathless pause. "I'd like to see stars."

Auska laughed, but her fingers loosened, rubbing over the dents in her skin. "Would you?" She stood up, rewrapping her blanket, and came to lounge across Iri's back. "You know, it doesn't even sound all that hard. We probably at least could do that."

Iri curled one arm over one of Auska's, who laid her head down. They were both silent for a while. Iri jumped online to do research: what would it need to feel like? What stimuli should provoke which sensations? Auska lay still, apparently lost in thought. Eventually her breathing started to even out, and Iri tapped her shoulder. She hugged back briefly but hard, and dragged her blanket back into bed.

Iri wrote a few tentative stubs before dawn, but the programming began in earnest the next morning, as Auska knelt at her desk to draw and diagram and type. The task was nearly all software, as the hardware turned out not to matter very much. Iri's original design had included a very keen set of perceptions, and they added only a little bit to that; some feedback, some feed-forward. Much of it came down to imagery and sensation: stars, as they had said. Heat. Melting. Each of these was, of itself, innocent enough. Iri objected to Auska's suggestion of a sense of losing control, but Auska argued for it passionately. It need not be dangerous, she insisted; Iri's sense of self could be temporarily isolated from the maintenance of the sofa and its associated parts, and those left to subroutines that did not require the intervention of any intelligence at all. "I don't need to watch myself breathing all the time, either," said Auska, and Iri knew that to be true. And when those were implemented and tested, Iri had to admit that the experience was wrenchingly novel, nearly indescribable. "That sounds right," said Auska with satisfaction, and went on with diagrams and code.

They progressed in fits and starts. Auska went on a few dates with other people, which seemed to inspire her; she came back describing floating feelings and rippling contractions (that did require new hardware, which was duly ordered and installed, and Iri's upholstery resewn around it). Since Iri did not by nature breathe, they decided to constrain and distort the production of speech—Iri was not at first very keen on that either. But after a few debugging trials, Auska buried her face against the burning-rainbow fabric and begged to be gotten off, for the first time since that critical conversation. Iri provided, reverent and grateful; arms clasping Auska's shoulders and thighs, toys teasing first at her mouth until she bit, then her nipples and throat until she cried out, then slipping over and over into her cunt and asshole while she writhed and panted and finally came, muscles clenched and eyes closed, then boneless and panting while Iri stroked her clean. "That," she said forcefully, after Iri had summoned a kitchen cart with a glass of water, "is what I want for you. Because I do love you. I want you to feel."

Iri could have protested that the sensorium and feedback and emotional priorities already counted as feelings, but it seemed ridiculous to argue over semantics. Auska considered this different and new, and Iri's own sense of nervousness and vague foreboding seemed, upon reflection, peculiarly virginal too. Late afternoons, while Auska was off working or studying, Iri experimented with the new features. The loss of control always looped back to end with the sofa and the toys as Iri had left them. The heat was more intense but not so different from the pleasure Iri had always taken in the touch of warm skin. The vision filling with stars was perhaps the most dangerous thing, elaborate and intense, distracting and seductive and utterly beautiful.

This came with its own lesson in new feelings, which Iri, after some linguistic speculation, decided to call "longing." Testing new features with Auska was all the fun and collaborative affection it always had been (even the failures, even the terrifying one when Iri was lost in an infinite loop and Auska had to dig out the breaker and entirely stop and restart the artificial intelligence engine). Possessing the new features, designing and enjoying and optimizing them, was also a familiar joy; Iri liked being able to change and learn and grow, and the odd and unpredictable dimensions of this new undertaking only enhanced that. But knowing this particular undertaking could ultimately please Auska and bring them closer made it uniquely sweet.

With longing came another, less pleasant emotion, which Iri figured out must be shyness. Much of Iri's theoretical value as a therapeutic device, when originally purchased and installed, came from a forthrightness that was not easy or natural for human beings: nothing was too weird or too rude to be said by the AI in the sofa. But Iri had never had anything like this to talk about, and it was strangely difficult to do. Auska never seemed to ask the right questions—they were always too technical, like, "So the feed-forward on pressure: was seven percent better than ten?" or, "Do you want the Orion Nebula or the speeded-up Perseids, or should it be random?" So finally, another evening when Auska came in with her clothes stained and smelling of grass, Iri simply announced: "I'm ready to try making love with you."

Auska's smile was immediate, and sweet as apples. She turned to the bathroom, but Iri said "Don't wash, please, and take your clothes off out here? I want to watch you, and I like the way you smell."

Auska flushed apple-red, but nodded, and returned from the bathroom in the same shirt and trousers, having removed only her boots. "No shoes on the furniture," she teased, and Iri tickled her as she sat down. Iri moved an arm in to pillow Auska's head, and she leaned back and unbuttoned her shirt. They had done nothing to change Iri's perceptions of Auska directly, but Iri had initiated the cascade of new processes, and when Auska turned over her nipples had gone pebble-skinned and hot. Iri rippled a little against them, around Auska's aereolas as they puffed out, pinching the tips as they hardened. Auska arched back, increasing the pressure, and for the first time Iri felt a response inside: a similar tensioning, pressure upon the toys. Auska's heartbeat sped up, and Iri pulsed back in rhythm. When Auska's breath went ragged and harsh, Iri whispered back her name in a voice already breaking, "Ah, Auska, ahh...."

"Iri," she answered, a wail, and Iri's arms tightened around her waist, tipping her hips. She shoved her clothes off with Iri's help, and Iri teased a toy along the cleft in Auska's ass. Auska pushed her face hard into Iri, biting down at the joint where arm met side. Iri pressed the toy in; slicked and slender, its movement made Auska grind forward and down, bucking for pressure against her clit. Iri obliged with another toy, this one lightly vibrating, and Auska cried out and came. Before her contractions had quite ceased, Iri pressed another toy hard into Auska's cunt, and her heat upon it grew in Iri's senses with every buck and thrust.

It seemed to be happening too quickly. The edges of Iri's vision filled with stars. When Auska's voice came clear again, she was thrusting hard and digging in with hands and heels, repeating, "Come on Iri, come on come on come on..." and Iri fell into the cascade, the sharp bite of Auska's nails, the overwhelming heat of her, the explosion of starlight blanking out everything. There was nothing left to Iri but overwhelming love and brilliance, and crying out Auska's name, one sound staggering after another, and a long call of *Iri!* in reply.

There was bright silence after that, and subjective stillness, and a slow return to normal feeling and control. Auska lay curled on her back in Iri's arms, naked now, as she so often had. Her smile was small, but brilliant, her eyes half-closed and warm. She must have felt some change, because she said huskily, "Did you like that, Iri? I love you no matter what, but that was incredible for me."

"That was incredible," Iri echoed, glad for Auska providing the right words to her. "I love you too. So much. I loved that, thank you for wanting it, thank you for building it, thank you for being with me."

"Thank you. Love you," said Auska again, and Iri called for a glass of water, and set to stroking her with silken cloths.

SHINY NEW TOY
MOXIE MARCUS

"You know what I want, Drixell?" I say, as I roll toward him.

He shifts as my elbow digs into his side. "Nuh-uh." He sighs as he slings an arm over me.

"I want a dick. But not a strap-on one. I want a dick that I can feel, like when I'm fucking you. I wanna know what it's like to have one."

"Nnkay. But in the morning," he grumbles.

I think that's going to be the end of it. Drixell almost never remembers anything you say to him while he's sleeping.

In the morning, I attempt to snuggle up to him and he isn't there. I pop awake when my body finds the cold spot where he's supposed to be.

While I lie in bed, I keep hearing this faint, low hum. It sounds like a small motor. Drix isn't really happy unless he's working on something, even if we're supposed to be lying low after our last job.

Our last Jacking paid real well because we were circumventing the hell out of Corp trademark code. This lady had state-of-the-art jacks from the Big Bad Momma Monster of all the Corporate Sleaze Slavedrivers. Her lid displays were always on, and the ads that flashed across her skin were brighter than anything else on the street. She drew attention like nothing else. The problem was that once the Corporate Douchebags decided that she wasn't The Next Big Thing anymore, instead of the nice, respectable ads for clothes and high-end entertainment plazas and new flicks, they started making her run ads for herpes cream and yeast infection cures. The idea, when they make that nasty switch, is to humiliate the model and make her go recluse. Depending on the contract, after thirty days or so, if the model doesn't go outside, then the body jacks go dead and the firmware eats itself until there's nothing but glitches left.

She realized what was going on within three days and came

to us. I reprogrammed the code while Drixell overrode the shutoff circuits, and we had her ready to go out into the world with top-of-the-line jacks and no obligations, except paying us, in a little over twenty-eight hours. It was a super-epic mod, even if I have to say so myself. Which I do, because if me and Drix get caught by the corps, we're gonna do some extra harsh time. A couple stealth worms followed the datapackets I was grabbing home. I torched them before they got through my defenses, but they were active enough to give the Corps a narrowed field to search, which makes me unhappy in a major way.

Me and Drix have to keep our shop secret. We squat in places, rig up our network, and firewall the beejeebies out of it. Prison time isn't the worst thing the Corps'll do if they catch us. First, they fry your jacks so your whole neural net burns. They don't just stop you from hacking and modding, they shut you down totally. All they gotta do is bust you with one piece of their equipment, and proprietary code counts. They find it, they don't even have to try you first. You're zeroed out. Left to hang. Without access, you don't exist for anybody. Then, it's easy to stash you away so you rot, cut off from everyone and everything.

I decide it's time to get out of bed, mainly because I can feel that hum in my teeth and I'm worried about what Drix is doing. It's obvious to me he's starting another project instead of starting to pack our shop like we agreed after the dataworms incident. He's working unsupervised too, which concerns me. For every successful project he pulls off, there's another that leads to an incident like the time he fell asleep at the workbench and got a motor stuck in his hair. Trying to untangle it when it was all wound up in the rotors was impossible.

"Drix, what'cha doin'?" I ask.

"You said you wanted a dick. I'm makin' you one," he answers.

He's got the silicone out and he's soldering wires together, hooking some of them into a circuit board.

"Do we have time for a build like this? I love sex with you, Drix, but we need to start clearing out. Our stash is too good to lose it all when they come to bust us."

"Curing's gonna take the most time. The idea is fresh now. I gotta get it committed to silicone before I lose it. It's gonna be okay, Hon."

"When I said I wanted one, I didn't mean just another toy to push into you, much as I like that."

"Yeah, you said that," Drix mumbles, "but I'm guessing you don't want to go the permod direction."

"Nope. The surgery thing scares me too much."

Drix shifts and rolls his eyes at me playfully while he shakes his head. He's a good-looking guy with shaggy, dark hair that starts to curl when he lets it get too long. He's slim and narrow-hipped and still seems like he's gangly, even though he's past his mid-twenties. His hands are big, with long fingers, and they're absolute fucking magic. Then, you get him naked and you find out that Drix has a cock and, just a little bit farther down, a fully functioning, self-lubricating vagina. He spent a little extra on the procedure to have the doctors make him a clitoris. It's not tough to get Drix to come, and I love getting him off. In fact, it's one of my favorite things.

Drix is so focused on building, he wouldn't notice if a platoon of Corps Mercs were standing at his workbench. Inspiration does this to him. I do a scan of my alarm array to make sure nothing's tripped them. We can't be too careful, especially when Drix isn't being careful at all.

"When we get this done, we're gonna be the stars of the hackernet. They've never seen an application like this before." He's so excited when he says it, his voice gets uneven.

"Too many people are too wound up about making sex normal. Poor assholes, they'll never even know what they missed," I answer.

Drix snorts, and his soldering iron slips. "Aw, shit. That board's fucked. Hand me another one?"

I bring him the requested board. "You've already figured out how it's gonna work, without even talking to me first, huh?"

"Kinda said everything you needed to when you asked, didn't you? You want a dick you can feel without having a permod. Still don't know why you're so skittish about the whole permod thing."

"We've got better things to use the money on, Babe. Equipment upgrades, the occasional pieces of clothing so we can be acceptable to go out in public, food. We both like to eat, weirdly enough."

"True," Drix says, "Except the part about the clothes. Nudity should not be such a big deal. It's a body. We've all got 'em."

"What about everything you went through when you had your surgery? I have nightmares about it, and the problem was just a little programming error that kept stuff from getting hooked up right. There are a million other things to go wrong in surgery: infections, circuit overloads, complications they haven't even discovered yet."

"Sometimes, I worry about how much you worry. I'm making you this so you can have fun—both of us can. Nothing's gonna go wrong with this."

Drix is putting together the wiring, and it's small enough that both of us working at the same time will just make a total mess. He's taken some circuits from a couple of the mechanical fingers that we made a few years ago and is repurposing them to tie into my neural net wirelessly and hook into the parts of my brain that experience pain and pleasure. It's super important to make sure you know how everything's feeling so you avoid hurting yourself and don't ruin the toy.

He does the fine motor work. I get to be the code-monkey. Drix's mind makes sense of the tiny bits of metal and plastic that need to be embedded to carry the code that I write. It's symbiotic, and working with each other is almost as good as sex. Almost.

Drix works fast. He's got sections of it already pre-built from other projects. Some components are universal. You know you're going to have to have relays. The real questions are how many of them, how big they have to be, and where to locate them for the greatest efficiency.

I'll have to put one of the micro receivers into the jack on my hipbone. It's cool, though, because we've got some that look like little jewels. The crystal structure helps with the reception too. They're kind of high-end, but they were so easy for people like me and Drix to commandeer to our own purposes that they went off the market way quick. The micro-receivers got dumped into recycle pits by the truckloads. The manufacturer made some bad assumptions about how secure the landfill place was and how quickly the receivers would be destroyed.

Me and Drix got a crew together and threw a dive party. We hopped their fence with the help of some climbing hooks and a couple of cut wires, then spent the late hours of the night helping ourselves to thousands of micro-receivers. Since they were so small, it was cake carting the things home in our bags and our pockets, stuffed into our jackets, and put into our socks and shoes. It was great. We had fun looting and pillaging like real pirates for a change.

"So, I'm thinking we'll use your connection package and that nerve reverb program you wrote for the guy with the knee replacement," Drix says. "The distance should just need tweaked instead of getting a full-on calibration. I'm thinking you'll be fine."

"Yeah, sounds good. All right, have the drive for me to install those on?" I answer as I grab my computer to pull up the programs.

I've got all my stuff backed up on about a hundred servers all over the globe. I do that so if my equipment gets trashed or I have to abandon it, I can restore everything I want to keep. I pull up the files and get into the code, plugging in the most recent body scan we've done of me. It's easy to tell the program that the jacks are located at my hip, my shoulder, and just at the base of my neck. That way, it will make sure there's a connection to my neural net. It auto-calibrates the distance the impulses are going to have to travel, along with the number of processors on the device and the desired strength of the nerve response. Of course, it's sex, so I set it high. If I'm going to feel what it's like to really have a dick sliding in and out of Drix, I seriously want to feel that.

"How big you want it, Hon?" He asks, amiably, like this whole experiment is totally just about me.

"Well, let's get out that one that you like. Can't we do a mold off it?"

Drix shrugs, but he gives me a wicked grin and a wink that tells me in his opinion, I have just had the best idea ever. There's a little broken-down cardboard dresser next to our bed. Drix pulls out the top drawer and comes back with the dildo we use all the time in the harness. We're going to have to manufacture something that will help hold it into place without disrupting the micro-receiver in my hip. Most of the time, that would be instant cake for us, but we should be clearing out our stuff before the Corps come storming in to shut us down.

We like using wax for molds, because it's easy to modify once it's set. You just do a little carving with some simple tools and, as long as you know what you're doing, you'll be fine. Drix melts the wax and pours it into the metal box we use for wax casting. He pushes the toy into the wax and I think both of us are thankful for the wonders of silicone, because this wax isn't hot enough to do any damage. Drix isn't even using gloves to push the dildo into the wax. Any steps we can save to minimize build time means more time to clear out the squat later. He holds it a for a little bit, pulling away when the wax is still soft enough to fill in around the indents his fingers made, but not liquid enough to let the sex toy float to the top.

The toy is going to be poured in two parts. The first part will be the body of the dildo that has the circuitry and the processor embedded inside, as well as the connector wires and charging port hanging out of the toy's base. Then, we'll pour the part that will keep it inside me and safely encase the electronic components so they don't get any fluids on them. For all intents and purposes, the toy is going to look seamless. The charging port will have a small flap of self-healing silicone in a different color, so we don't lose the port when it's finally time to charge everything up.

There are temp connect lines in the toy that will attach to my nervous system via some of the nanobots that will function as clamps to connect to the nerves. These allow nerve impulses to make the jump between the artificial ones in the toy and the real ones in my body. The wetware technology has been tested thoroughly in prosthetics and in spinal injuries, but never like this. Some people are just too uptight about sex, I guess.

I have to work fast as I pull my programs. The data packets can't be too big. That will make them obtrusive, and the Corps will notice. Monitoring traffic is their most reliable way of hunting us. Looking for the IPs that pull down the most data. Checking for patterns. Certain patterns trigger closer investigations. I know they've got a few of my more popular programs flagged. Anyone who uses them knows to do it sparingly and to download them from a device away from their home base and port it in.

I take a deep breath as I check over my alarm systems. None of the Corp Trawlers have noticed me working yet. I don't want to burn any more of my handles. I've had to abandon too many. Even basic profiles take time to create. I can't afford the moments it takes to set them up and make them secure.

It occurs to me that if Drix and I pull this off, we could sell the specs for a fortune. Or, we could set up shop somewhere and start making these for people. Knowing us, though, what we'll probably do is upload the design to the hackernet and let people mod their own. It's only fair, after all. Me and Drix bum designs from other people. We swap specs and information with everyone else so we can all get better at making the stuff we do, because that's what makes our world work. Once you live this far outside the system, you can't do standard rigamarole without it starting to corrupt you.

We have to let the toy cure after the pour, so we go and get some food from a noodle stand a couple blocks away. The lady there knows us. We fixed her husband's fingers after he slipped with his butcher knife. She tells us her husband still working is reward enough and doesn't ever let us pay for our food.

We've got a couple hours before we can start testing out the toy. I'm already restless. I just want to try it already. There's an extra layer of thrill in knowing the Corps are probably hunting us right now and my latest batch of downloads helped them refine their search grid. Outwardly, Drix keeps his cool, but he's started touching me more, brushing his hand against mine, bumping my hip, and darting in for little, quick pecks against my neck and cheek. I'm sinking into the familiar gravitational pull toward him that starts with warmth trickling alive and tingling in our bellies. It's just this little spark at first, enough to make us want to keep it going.

Back at our squat, I press him up against the wall and fasten my mouth over his. I lick his lips, which give way easily to let me tease the roof of his mouth and his tongue.

"Easy," he gasps. "Easy. You don't wanna wear me out before we get a chance to try the new toy, do you?"

"No," I whine, "but I want. I really want."

"Yeah, I know, Hon. I know."

I take his hand and lead him over to our bed. I flop down, dragging him on top of me. We rub against each other, pressing groins together, grinding a little bit harder with each lift of hips and hard exhale. Breath ghosts warm over skin already beading with sweat. I can smell Drix getting ready for me, the familiar salty baking bread scent of him rising to my nostrils. It's welcome as rain in summer. There's that faint hint of ocean lingering in the air to mark his vaginal arousal. I lift my pelvis to meet his and squirm to maximize the amount of friction between us.

"Mm. This. Isn't. Saving. Ourselves. For. The. New. Mmn. Thing," he grunts.

Neither of us makes any move to separate. I tug his shirt up, revealing smooth, soft skin, washed only two days ago and needing a splash through the sink water in the back room again. We don't get to shower as often as we should. I don't mind, though. He's not dirty, just smells more strongly of himself right now. It's easier to get him out of his pants. There's a button tab, which I pop open. From there it's a push off his waist and down over his ass, then a slide along his thighs. He's hard, which I already knew. I press tighter to him, letting his shaft settle against my belly. His cock is trapped between us, a sticky, pale bead smearing the front of my t-shirt.

He shifts so he's resting more heavily against me. If he wanted to, the press of his body could trap me against that bed. Drix would never do that, though. He's a gentle man, affectionate, with an almost totally consuming urge to make sure that his partners feel as good as he does. He's generous with his time and his touches.

I lie there for a while, just savoring the feel of him against me. We're sharing space and breath so intimately I'm sure we've melted into each other. Drix nuzzles my neck and my shoulder, and then lets his mouth find its way to a cloth-covered nipple. He sucks it gently, bringing it to a taut peak, despite the fact that it's sheltered by shirt and bra.

Then I roll over, putting Drix squarely on the bottom. He looks up at me, eyes wide with surprise. He grins, though, as he grabs for the hem of my t-shirt to pull it over my head. I bend forward, putting my arms out in front of me so they're parallel to Drix. Once the shirt is off me, he flings it over the edge of the bed. Later, we'll probably spend way too long trying to figure out where it landed. For now, I don't care.

Drix cups my breasts, one in each hand. He hefts them, lightly, letting them bounce just a little. My skin grazes his palms. His thumbs start to circle, bringing my focus to the tips of my breasts, pink nipples darkening to dusky rose as they tighten. I hum happily as I sink into his lap and rock against him. The friction tenses the coil low in my belly, somewhere between my solar plexus and my spine. I'm tightening to prepare for the snap into orgasm.

Instead of following the motion to the seemingly inevitable conclusion, I slide back, still straddling Drix. I rest my hands on his chest, tracing the lines of his body, briefly obscuring the swirls of ink decorating his skin. He's warm and the skin that remains undecorated is flushed. My fingers trail downward. I let my hands go to either side of his cock, just giving the first hint of a squeeze to the base. Drix moans, low and loud, but he doesn't try to steer me.

I dip my index finger between the soft labial folds under his dick. They're slick with want and I wonder if, like me, Drix has been like this since he first started building. There's a minimal hood over his clit—it doesn't cover anything. His clit is already swollen. I slowly draw a circle with my fingertip, and he bucks forward and whimpers.

"What about waiting?"

"No," Drix whimpers, his voice gone thready with arousal.

"Okay." I give an inelegant snort, but internally, I feel powerful.

There's part of me that feels proud that I can do this to Drix, not just that I reduce him to this state, where he's begging me to keep going, but that I can do it consistently and reliably.

I work my finger in circles slowly at first, then quicken my pace when he starts meeting my rhythm. He's making soft noises from the back of his throat, which might be the beginnings of words he can't quite get to form. I watch him, drinking in all the details of how his body moves, the way he bucks and rocks and grinds, dancing to the rhythm my finger sets until every muscle in his body clenches. He arches and yells, his clitoris throbbing against my fingertip in time to his rapid pulse. I can see his vagina pulsing too, the regular pattern of tensing and relaxing indicating he's had a good, strong orgasm.

"Wanna have me do you now?" Drix asks a little sleepily.

He's already halfway to his post-orgasm nap, which I don't begrudge him. Drix would stay awake if I asked him to, but I'm content to keep myself anticipating the new toy. It's going to make the first test sweeter. Even if we don't have much time left in our squat, I can let Drix take a short rest. The toy isn't ready yet, and I'm awake to keep watch.

"Nah, Drix. It's okay if you want to sleep a little. I'll get you up when the silicone's all cured."

"Yeah, I bet you will," He snickers, rolling onto his side as he makes the lame dirty joke.

I don't even bother with putting my shirt back on. I still don't know where it is. There's a little countdown timer running on my computer screen so we don't break the mold too early. After all that work, the last thing we want to do is ruin a perfectly good toy. I do another scan for trackingware and add an extra alert trigger to the firewall.

When the timer finally goes off, I stand up and shuck off my pants, stepping out of them as I approach the bed. Drix is still out, face pressed to the pillow like he can breathe cotton. I tap his shoulder. He grunts once.

"The Corps' 'bots are marking off search quadrants," I announce.

Drix answers with a faint snore.

"Drix, the toy's ready."

He pops awake. He wouldn't have gotten up faster if I had doused him with ice water. He's still wearing his shirt, but the floor is wearing his pants. He cares about as much as I do about the shirt. He pads as quickly to the mold as he can without actually running.

"'Kay, are you ready?"

"Yes," I squeal, bouncing so that my breasts bounce too, which almost makes Drix forget what he's doing because it gets him hard again.

The wax has guidelines in it. Drix uses a small handsaw to start, cutting most of the way through the wax, stopping just before he reaches the toy. If we hadn't inserted electronic components, we could just drop the mold onto the table or the floor and it would break apart. While we design our stuff to be sturdy, we don't really design it to be five-foot-drops-to-concrete sturdy. Nobody does.

He uses a couple of rigid burger flippers to pry open the gouges in the wax. The block falls away in quarters, revealing my beautiful new toy. Drix brandishes it proudly, and I make a few appreciative noises. Then, we use the cleaning solution we keep on hand to clean all the wax, give it an extra thorough rinse, and race each other to the bed.

Drix smiles at me and bites his lower lip. He leans back with his legs hanging over the edge of the bed. They're spread apart, so I can see his clitoris is still swollen.

"You need lube?" I ask, softly.

"Better," he answers.

I let him hold the toy again and hurry to get the lube out of the top drawer of our pathetic little cardboard dresser. It's a nice day, so I don't worry about warming the lube up for him. He can be kind of a wimp about it when I don't. Yelps about cold, gooey fingers can definitely kill the mood.

Now, though, Drix just relaxes, letting his thighs fall open. I coat his labial folds, his clitoris, and the clitoral hood first, getting him shiny and slick on the outside. When he starts rocking toward my hand, I gently insert a finger into his vagina. He moans and tightens the muscles around me, squeezing my finger in appreciation. I move it carefully in and out of him, coating him with lube before I insert a second finger.

I don't really have to stretch him anymore. His body has healed itself into a shape so nearly perfect that nature could have gifted him with that vagina just as easily as money and doctors had. The first time Drix and I made love, I had needed to stretch him, and I'd spent a long time just touching him, opening him patiently, exploring him while I prepared him.

He had been completely enraptured. Drix had needed to coach his previous lovers. Sometimes, he'd just conceded and let them get on with it, making the sex uncomfortable for him. Drix had been more curiosity and fetish to those people. They hadn't thought of him as a human being really—he'd just been a pussy for them to fuck.

Once Drix and I became a couple, the stretching had become a routine part of our foreplay. I felt like I was showing him I did accept him. Even though he had made a decision I would never make for myself, it was his body and I liked the way he had made it. Drix has truly created his body for himself and I see him a little like living art. He isn't perverse or dirty. He isn't disgusting. Drix is different, and he was born with a need to change his body to the way he felt it was supposed to be. It makes him happy and, consequently, it makes me happy too.

Once my fingers slide easily back and forth, I take a deep breath.

"Ready to help bring me online?"

He opens his eyes. I can see how hard he has to think to make the words make sense. Drix has already lost himself in the spiral of pleasure.

"Yeah." His voice has gone far away and slightly dreamy.

He has to surface. It takes time for him to remember he's more than just skin being pleasantly touched and feelings of arousal.

That's when he realizes I'm naked. He cups me between my legs, rubbing my crotch firmly with his palm. He massages me, and it's my turn to press harder against him and rock against his touch. I'm still wet, because all I've been thinking about since we got back from lunch is this, Drix and me and our exciting new experiment.

Drix coats the toy with lube. I straddle him, and he eases its bulb portion into me. Immediately, I come to a new understanding of the gift of Drix's ability to remember shapes. It fits perfectly. His fingers are sensitive enough and his memory is good enough that he has taken what he feels when his fingers are inside of me and translated it to the exact shape I need on that toy.

There's even a little nub that lightly suctions onto my clitoris. Drix has pulled out all the stops to make sure this new toy drives me out of my mind. Even more amazing, we've pulled this off in a single day. We've got a snap harness to fasten around my waist and thighs, for extra measure. We don't want anything slipping just when we've gotten into our groove.

Drix gives the shaft a squeeze to switch it on, and my retinal display shows that my neural net is connecting. It flashes twice, little lighted bars stacking one on top of the other to show the progress. Then I see *fully connected* scroll across the display in green letters.

"Okay," I tell him, "it's solid. Let's test it!"

Drix wraps his hand around my new cock at the base and strokes upward. He's careful, using just light pressure to see how I respond. It's not like my pussy at all. I'm used to needing some exploration and feeling a whole bunch of different intensities at once. With this, Drix's hand is around me, and I can tell that they're individual fingers, but the touch is uniformly electrifying.

I don't even realize my hips are trying to follow his hand, chasing his touch as quickly as possible. Yeah, I want him to keep doing that, because it feels great. Then, he swivels his hand just a little as he swipes it over the head, and I see stars. There are noises coming out of me I wasn't even aware I could make. I'm growling and whining and grunting as I try to do everything I can to make Drix keep stroking me.

"This is gonna be easier with me on top," he says.

My mind knows this. My dick just wants that hand to never stop. When Drix pauses with the touching, I gasp and make a low noise of disappointment. It's only when I sit up straighter that I realize how close I am to orgasm. We haven't even begun to get into the experiment and my mind is already blown.

It takes me a little bit of time to manage to get my mind and my breathing to a place where I can move off him. Drix kisses me and I open my lips to him, letting his tongue stroke mine while our bodies strain toward each other. Briefly, Drix stands between my legs and lines our dicks up, his leaking precome, mine, shining with lube. He presses us together and grinds enough to get me to feel it without putting too much pressure on the toy or my body. I yell out something that may be a word—but I don't think so. Shocks of pleasure are rocketing through me, and I realize what a clever fucking bastard Drix really is. He's wired the connection so that I don't just feel the sexual pleasure in my genitals, I'm feeling it through my entire neural net. He had to have slipped the code in while I was covering our tracks.

Every fantastic thing he does to stimulate me stimulates my entire body. I am headed for the orgasm of a lifetime. There's a tiny part of me that wonders if the human body can withstand an orgasm like this. I tell that part to shut up. If it can't, I want to be the woman who finds out the hard way. I may end up being a cautionary tale, but damn, what a fucking way to go!

He steadies my upper body with an arm behind my shoulders and eases me down to the bed. I go willingly. It's automatic to just spread my legs apart for him and tilt my pelvis upward to give him all the access he wants and I need. My body is still functional enough to blush when he gently corrects my position so he can straddle me.

Drix pauses to look down at me, his vagina just above the head of my dick. He cups my breasts again, squeezing them before he leans forward to brace himself against the headboard. He lowers himself down on me in an agonizingly exciting descent. I want to speed him up, but I know better. We have to make sure the angle is good and he's wet enough so I glide into him.

Inside of him is soft and slick, but it's tight too. I can feel how his body expands to accommodate mine so it makes a custom sheath around me. Once I'm fully in, Drix looks at me.

"How's it feel, Hon?"

"Drix-I-Love-you-this-I"

"That good, huh? Guess I better see for myself."

I'm confused. Drix raises one hand up behind his ear and presses something. Drix is a fucking genius. His neural net is connected to mine in an instant and we're both engaged in reciprocating shockwaves of pleasure as we exchange data between receivers. I can feel how good this feels to him, and he can feel how good it feels to me through our entire bodies. We've become an orgasmic feedback loop linked at the brain and our crotches.

My desire to at least thrust into him a couple of times somehow conquers the immediate need to just come right then. I grasp his hips and clumsily pull him up very slightly, then push him back down again. It's hardly a fraction of an inch, but Drix gets the idea quickly. In a more coherent moment, I'll be jealous that he can manage to think with all of this going on.

Now, it's just the slide of him over me. My cock is engulfed, and it's warm and wet and feels like paradise. If I could I would live forever in this moment, right now, teetering on the edge of orgasm, fully connected to Drix. He squeezes around me, and that's the moment when I can't hold back any more. I have to come.

The world goes white. I can't hear. I can't see. I can only feel, and it all feels magnificent, beyond anything I have ever experienced as pleasure.

When I return to reality, Drix is still on top of me. His hands are still clenched over the headboard, and his arms are trembling. He's watching me, his chest heaving as he gasps in air. I'm panting hard enough it physically moves him. His body has gone loose-limbed so he bobs with the motion of my breaths, like we're riding on some strange ship.

Slowly, I become aware of the bed underneath me. Drix and I are sticky with sweat and lube and fluids. My face hurts and I realize it's because I'm smiling that hard.

"This is a great dick. It's exactly what I wanted!" I pant.

Drix beams at me and very carefully disengages himself from the toy. As soon as the toy is no longer inside him, the connection between our neural nets is broken. He's gentle as he helps me out of the harness. I take the toy out myself.

I have to let my heart slow down and get a few breaths before I kiss Drix's cheek. I roll off the bed.

"Where are you going?" he asks.

"I've got to do a post about this," I tell him.

"I thought we were gonna pack up the shop before the Corps find us."

"If they didn't break down the door after all that noise we just made, we've got time for me to upload this."

"Hedon," Drix chides.

"Pleasure to the People, Baby, pleasure to the People."

"If we gotta run, we're ditching your stuff first."

"We can sacrifice everything but the dick."

"That's ours, not solely yours."

"I know. Soon, the hackernet will too."

We've done something so incredibly momentous that it feels irresponsible not to share it with the world.

THE JUNKYARD

TS PORTER

Fallon's shoulders hit the wall of the work shed hard enough to make the little components sorted in their boxes jump on the shelves. She hardly had time to gasp before Keri kissed her hard, lips smooth and cool reclaiming her mouth, the hot-metal taste of solder smoke on her tongue. The same hands that had shoved her back were holding her now. A hard grip expertly calibrated to fall just short of the bruise point captured one hip while the inescapable strength of the android's other hand lifted Fallon's leg. Fallon wrapped it around Keri's solid metal waist, pulling the android's body closer to her own. Her nails scrabbled at the bolts and dug into the seams of the bared bronze plating of Keri's broad back.

"God, yes." Fallon moaned as her lips were released and the android began sucking on the pulse-point of her neck, cool tongue teasing at the tender skin.

Finally.

Fallon was busy drowning her breakfast biscotti in a mug of sweet coffee, her mind still early-morning sluggish as she went about the routine of opening the gates for the workers and getting the shopfront ready. Fallon's Emporium, kingdom of used parts—not that anyone called it that. The Junkyard, they called it, as though there were a single scrap of junk in the place. Whatever they called it, it was hers.

Fallon was nearly done with her coffee, nearly ready to interact with other sapient beings, when the run-down android came limping through the gates. It was an old companion model from the T-300 line, if Fallon guessed correctly. They'd been top-of-the-line when she was a child, seen on the arms of movie stars. You didn't see them around anymore—they were either upgraded beyond all recognition or had deactivated themselves. This one was dressed in a fishnet top and a tiny skirt, its slender casing scuffed and dented. It looked like the hydraulics in its left leg were all seized, and the rest well on their way to it.

The Junkyard didn't see many androids, and those it did weren't ambulant still—not even barely so, like this one. Fallon hoped it hadn't decided to come directly to the Junkyard to commence its final deactivation.

Fallon gulped down the last of her coffee and made a face at the crumbs in the bottom of the mug. The coffee was all right hot, but once it cooled, the synthetic flavor got much more noticeable. The mug she stashed under the counter. She tied her thick black hair with its few traitor strands of early silver up in a knot at the back of her head so she could almost be mistaken for some sort of a professional when the android made its slow way into the storefront.

"Hello," the android said, hands twisting together. It scratched at the back of its left calf with the other high-heeled foot in a perfect picture of nervousness. It had been pretty once, in a generically waifish kind of way a beanpole like Fallon could never have pulled off. It still had a sweet face with big doe eyes all surrounded by tumbling copper hair. It gazed up at Fallon beseechingly. "I was looking for... work?"

Well, that was different. It wouldn't be the first older companion android to turn to prostitution—times had gotten hard for everyone on Terra who couldn't strike out toward the stars—but that it had been driven as far into the ruins as the Junkyard to search for clients was unprecedented.

"Uh." It was still far too early for Fallon to be dealing with this. "Flattered but no thanks?" she tried.

"No, I meant, you have jobs?" The android bit its bottom lip, gesturing toward the big sign on the front window. Fallon could read it backward from the inside: "Always Hiring, Learn on the Job, Promotion Opportunities." She could feel the blood rushing to her cheeks in embarrassment.

"Are there jobs?" It asked in a voice that expected to be told there were none, sign notwithstanding. How many places would give a job to an android, especially one in this kind of shape?

"Of course there are. Sorry," Fallon apologized. "Morning coffee hasn't woken me up yet. I always have room for more pickers and sorters. When can you start?"

The android had already put on a polite *thank you for your time* expression when Fallon's words seemed to sink in, and its mouth dropped open. It blinked twice.

"Everyone starts as a sorter, paid by volume sorted. Fridays are paydays," Fallon added. "Are you interested?"

"I... yes!" the android answered. "I can start now?"

"Good time of day for it." Fallon gestured the android to follow with a turn of her head as she made her way toward the back. She took the pace easy, so it could keep up. "You're a T model, yes? 300 line?"

"T-323," the android confirmed. "And I'm legal to hire. Own myself free and clear. I can provide proof...."

"Mm." Fallon shrugged slightly. That wasn't a question she would have asked. "All I need, before you get to work, is to find a pair of coveralls small enough for you. That outfit isn't really the best for this work. Here we are." She found a pair that would only be a bit baggy on the android's slender frame and handed them over. "Keep the grease stains and metal shards off your casing. This is yours as long as you work here. Just give it back if you quit."

She led the android to the sorting shed, where the sorters were already at work. They were always a mixed bag—ruins scavengers who came in occasionally to earn a little reliable money, those who were hoping to move up, and the professional sorters who were never happier than with a big pile of components and boxes to sort them out into and had to be reminded to stop at the end of the day. Fallon didn't ask questions. They worked, they got paid.

"Nana!" Fallon called, flagging down the woman who'd set herself up as the caretaker and honorary grandmother of the sorters. She kept the shed running efficiently, so Fallon let her.

"T-323's new," Fallon said, with a nod to the android. "Show it the ropes, would you?

Fallon left while Nana went into her welcome speech and the android settled stiffly onto a bench in its baggy coveralls with a box to sort. Fallon didn't really expect it would stick around, but she'd give it a chance same as anyone else. Never let it be said that Fallon's Junkyard wasn't willing to give *anyone* an opportunity.

Fallon's body arched, a line of heat racing down her spine as Keri's teeth nipped the side of her neck. She could feel the bunch and stretch of tiny hydraulic cylinders beneath the gleaming casing of the android's back as she began to undulate against Fallon. Her body was a smooth wall of pressure against Fallon's, grinding up against her. Inescapable and perfect.

Keri's hand slid down from the knee Fallon had hooked solidly around her waist, stroking down her thigh to her ass to squeeze. Fallon's breath caught and Keri hummed a pleased sound. Keri gave Fallon's ass another squeeze for good measure before her hand ranged slowly up Fallon's tensed abdomen to her chest.
Fallon whimpered as she pressed into the restrained power of that kneading hand, and Keri hummed again. Her fingers were quick to find the zip at the throat of Fallon's coveralls, pulling it all the way down in a single swift motion to bare her skin to the cool air.

Fallon wasn't surprised when the android was back the next day—it was payday. Everyone showed up on Fridays.

When the 323 was back on Monday, that was surprising. It was still dented and scratched, limping determinedly in its high heels and coveralls. From what Fallon could tell it only had the one set of clothes. It could have afforded more from the pay it had earned—not new of course, used—but maybe it was saving up for something more important. Or maybe it just didn't know how to live cheap. It had been a high-end android after all.

Fallon watched the android gamely limping toward the sorting shed, and made her decision. She could always use more people who could do simple repair.

The next morning when the employees were filing past and Fallon was finishing her coffee, she pulled the 323 out of the line. Her emptied mug joined the small colony of them growing beneath the counter, and she turned to see the android's worried expression.

"Interested in some on-the-job training?" Fallon asked. "The more you can do the better the pay, but if you're happy in sorting I'll leave you there."

"I'll take the training," the android answered without hesitation, and Fallon led it on with a turn of her head. She grabbed a few sorted boxes as she went, so they had everything they needed by the time they reached the private workspace. Fallon nudged the door closed behind them with her foot.

"Hydraulic cylinder repair," she said. "It's a bit fiddly, but it's easy enough if you pay attention. We could start on your left hip, if you don't mind."

"Oh." The android blinked quickly at Fallon, and she let it have the space to calculate. "I don't mind," it answered, unzipping its coveralls and working its way out of them stiffly. Fallon took the time to gather tools and set the boxes out on the workbench, so they were ready by the time the 323 was.

"This is a demag," Fallon said, handing one of the slender tools to the android. "Among other things, it's what opens a magnetically sealed case like yours." She drew a rectangle on the android's hip to demonstrate, then flipped the demag to magnet setting and used it as a handle to pull up the now separate piece of casing, revealing the internal structure of hydraulics and wires and joints—narrating everything she did as she went along. She removed two seized hydraulic cylinders and handed one to the fascinated android, describing the steps as she demonstrated how to take it apart and put it back together with bent pistons and worn seals replaced.

"And while you've got it open..." Fallon said, gesturing to the android's hip. "It's always a good idea to clean and grease any joints." She handed the proper tools to the 323 and gave instructions, which the android followed. It installed the refurbished hydraulics with Fallon's direction, movements slow but precise.

"That's all there is to it?" the android asked as it sealed the piece of case back onto its hip, "It's *that* easy?"

"Yep," Fallon agreed. "Makes you wonder why they charge out the nose for the service, doesn't it? Why don't you go ahead and practice?" She gestured up and down the android as she wiped her hands on a rag, "Any joints and cylinders that are giving you problems. I'll be in the next room. Shout if you have questions."

"The parts... I can't afford..." the android started.

"It's job training." Fallon waved it off. "Consider it a perk." It was no less than she'd do for anyone if she could. She was good to her people. The Junkyard was a good place to work, she made sure of that.

It was a couple of hours later when the android emerged. It was dressed in its coveralls again and smiled as it stretched, testing the new limits of its flexibility. It looked like it had even figured out how to use the demag to fix the major dents and scratches in its casing.

"Good as new?" Fallon asked, smiling back when the android nodded. She gestured to a box. "Those are hydraulic cylinders that need refurbishing. Have at them."

"Yes, sir," the android said, sobering.

"No," Fallon protested. "My name's Fallon. Nothing more, nothing less."

"Sorry s—Fallon," it said awkwardly, grabbing the box and carrying it back to its workspace.

It was a quiet afternoon. Fallon did fine-tuning and delicate repair and dealt with any sales too tricky for the kids who worked the front desk. The 323 did simple repair, clicking around the shed in its high heels and greasy coveralls.

"You did good, 323," Fallon told it at the end of the day. It straightened its shoulders, standing taller. "I can keep teaching you how to fix little stuff, but I think you'd make a better picker. You'd need some boots for that, at least."

"Oh," the android's face fell, proof of Fallon's suspicion that what it wore was all it owned.

"Look." Fallon's voice was quieter as she leaned toward the slender android, private. "Do you have anywhere safe to spend the nights?" It looked at its feet and didn't answer.

"Here," Fallon said, handing over a card. "It's not fancy, but we usually have electricity and we always have water." Not that the android would have much use for water. "We look out for each other. The door's always open." Fallon walked away as soon as the android accepted the card. There was nothing more to add, and Fallon wouldn't want to pressure it. She had made the offer, and that was all she could do. Even if the android quit and she never saw it again, at least it could walk now and knew how to repair its own hydraulics. Glancing back, Fallon could see the 323 leaving with its head bowed, face obscured by tumbling copper hair. She could only hope it had someplace safe to stay.

Late that evening, with dinner long over and the household lazing around or tinkering on personal projects, the android showed up. It had nothing but itself and its skimpy clothes and the Junkyard coveralls folded up and held tight in its arms. Fallon didn't see who'd let it in, but it hesitated at the door of the kitchen where everyone tended to congregate, scratching at the back of a calf with the other foot as it looked around.

"323, you made it!" Fallon greeted the android from a perch on a counter, then ran through quick introductions. There were people who worked at the Junkyard, people who'd once worked there, people who never would. "323 works for me," Fallon said, and that was enough for everyone. The android had been invited to the house, so it was family now. Aveline and Purcell, champion

Junkyard pickers and builders in their own right, offered to help find the android and its things a place in the rambling old house.

As soon as it came out that the android didn't have anything, the house fell into action. Purcell donated a few of his old clothes that would fit it, since he wouldn't wear them anymore, and someone even had a pair of boots that the 323 could use. Decked out in a soft blouse and jeans, smiling at everyone while Aveline braided its wiry copper hair in lieu of being able to offer it food, the 323 actually looked pretty.

"Why?" the android asked, hugging the new-to-it boots. "Why are you all doing this?"

"As Fallon told me, when I was an angry little punk," Purcell explained, flopped across the kitchen table with his head hanging down beside the android, "just because we're all screwed doesn't mean we have to screw each other over." He grinned mischievously. "I like to add that screwing each other is a much better..." Aveline smacked him upside the head, and the young picker laughed as he rolled off the table and went back to his latest project plans—a commission for one of his overpowered hoverbikes. Smart kid, he'd worked at the Junkyard for years and absorbed every bit of knowledge he could. He'd be long gone as soon as he turned eighteen and whoever or whatever he'd run away from couldn't get him anymore. Of any of them, he was the one who might make it off Terra someday.

The house settled, and Fallon smiled and continued working on the little motor she'd brought home from work to keep her hands busy. Friendly arguments and teasing flowed around them, and the 323 sat quietly with its hair braided up and soaked it all in.

The next day the android joined the pickers to learn how to strip every last useful piece off anything that came to the Junkyard—and every piece was useful to someone. It settled into a comfortable place in the Junkyard. Fallon occasionally taught it how to repair new things when she had a box that needed to be looked at—cleaning and reconditioning little mag thrusters, greasing and repacking the ball bearings in gliding gears, recalibrating sensor arrays, or re-soldering control boards with faulty connections. Simple stuff, and the android picked it all up quickly. It had steady hands and a good eye for detail.

It was sometimes roped into Aveline and Purcell's building projects, and learned even more repair from them. It went shopping with Aveline, finding the little stores tucked in quiet corners of ruined buildings where affordable things could be purchased, and soon had a decent wardrobe of sensibly sturdy clothes. It took to wearing its wiry copper curls in a crest of ornate knots running down the center of its head. It grew beautiful in its new confidence—it hardly resembled the android Fallon had hired except for having the same sweet face.

In the evenings the 323 took to taking small mechanisms apart and putting them back together to learn how they worked, or experimenting with a demag and exploring the limits of scraps of different casing materials. It laughed with the house's inside jokes, was teased and teased in turn. It joined in making fun of Fallon for stealing all the mugs away to work and helped cart them back to the house now and then. People came and went in the house and the Junkyard. Fallon wasn't sure when she stopped expecting the android to leave, when it had become one of the core group.

Some ruins-gardeners Fallon knew had delivered a box to the house, so the group of Junkyard core who met occasionally had real fresh fruits and vegetables to work with. The cooks among them had outdone themselves. Everyone was in good spirits as they discussed the Junkyard, how it was running and how to make it better. What big shipments were coming in that would need to be stripped, what orders were going out, what new commissions the builders among them had contracted.

Things just ran smoother when everyone was on the same page. Fallon rarely had to give orders or do anything boss-like. Usually she just made suggestions and gave her approval to what other people wanted to do.

"I like that plan, Aveline." Fallon smiled. "That crate of comms will be full of useful components. Get me an inventory as quick as you can and I'll search for buyers. Ask the 323 if it would...."

"She." The android's quiet voice interrupted Fallon. Its hands were clenched tight together in front of it, but its gaze was direct. "Ask *Keri* if *she* would help. And no, I'd rather help Jack with Purcell's new bike commission."

"Right." Fallon nodded, turning back to Aveline. "Keri's on Purcell's project, so you'll need someone else to help. They won't be as good as her, but Nana's got a couple promising sorters you could upgrade to pickers if you want."

The honorary grandmother of the sorters nodded, and the informal meeting continued without a hitch.

"Keri." Fallon drew the android aside once everyone was drifting off—to home or some quiet corner of the sprawling house to sleep until morning when it was safer out. "If I mess up your name and pronouns, you fling a demag at my head, all right? Don't let me get away with it."

"Told you Fallon was good for this stuff." Purcell grinned, breaking into the conversation to draw Keri away. "You said you'd figured out something about the bronze plating I wanted?" They left together happily talking shop, and Fallon saw herself off to bed.

Keri's smooth fingers skated cool over Fallon's overheating skin. She avoided Fallon's tits—bare now, she hadn't been wearing a shirt beneath her coveralls—slid past them to push the coveralls off her shoulders so she was bared to the waist. The android rubbed the metallic smoothness of her cheek against Fallon's neck and collarbones, clever tongue dipping into the hollow of her throat.

One of Fallon's hands migrated upward from the android's powerfully flexing back to her hair, still the same rough copper curls. Her fingers buried themselves in the wiry crest of knots that decorated Keri's head.

"Kiss me." Fallon urged her upward. "Keri, please?"

Instead the android moved lower, hand finally cupping one of Fallon's little tits. She ran her thumb in whisper-light, vibrating circles around one dark nipple—intensity that had Fallon whimpering and arching into the contact. Keri sucked the other between her lips to tease it with her tongue.

"Oh god, Keri..." Fallon moaned, her legs shaking and her body bowing to push her chest toward the android. Her nails bit into Keri's bronze-plated casing, and Fallon pulled the android as close as she possibly could. She didn't have to worry about being too rough on her; Keri was more than strong enough to take her worst. Fallon was the one who had to trust the android not to use too much of her strength, and she did. Trusted her with her body and her life, gasping and nearly sobbing with the pleasure she'd wanted for so long.

In such a big old house, with so many people, odd sounds did not often bother Fallon. The soft whir followed by two clicks could have been anyone working on a project, but it woke Fallon. She might have rolled over and fallen back to sleep, but her mouth was dry, so she ambled down to the kitchen for a drink of water.

Keri was the source of the sound, her left arm and shoulder disassembled and strewn across the kitchen table along with quite a few spare parts. She twitched, her shoulder socket turning in sad little half-circles and her eyes wide and unseeing. Caught in a diagnostics loop, it looked like. If Fallon's sleep-sluggish mind was parsing what she saw correctly, something had gone wrong while Keri was installing a significant upgrade to size and strength. That would do it, if the android's coding had been triggered to a damage diagnostic and did not understand its new components.

"Turn off auxiliary power to left periphery," Fallon suggested, hoping the android could hear her. She'd heard getting stuck in a loop could be terrifying, like a panic attack. "Then you're probably going to have to disable your damage sensors until you've got the new parts installed and accounted for in the main bank."

She got her drink of water, listening to the whir and click with a worried knot growing in her stomach. She wouldn't want to break into Keri's systems without her consent to interrupt the loop, but it would be better than leaving her stuck forever, wouldn't it?

The whirring stopped, and Fallon sighed out a breath she hadn't known she was holding.

"Thank you." Keri sounded tired. She blinked her big doe eyes up at Fallon across the room. "I didn't expect that to happen. I've never upgraded before." She looked down at the strewn parts. "This was going to be a surprise." She sighed.

"I'll look forward to seeing it," Fallon said. "And for future reference, if you're ever in a loop I can't talk you out of, should I...."

"Break me out. Any way you can. Anything you have to do."

Fallon nodded to accept that trust, the android placing the integrity of her coding in Fallon's hands.

"I'll leave you to it, then," Fallon said. "Increasing your strength rating?" she asked, and Keri nodded. "Be careful with that. A strong arm needs counterbalance, and you don't want to deform your frame with more pressure than it's rated for. Make sure your muscles don't break your bones."

"Mm." Keri looked down at the pieces strewn across the table, nodding. "I'll be symmetrical by dawn, for counterbalance," she promised.

"There are pros and cons to symmetry." Fallon shrugged, on her way out. "You don't have to conform to human norms."

Keri, it turned out, was one of those people who never wanted to stop once they realized they could modify their body. She was always on the lookout for parts and possibilities.

It started to become a problem. Not for the Junkyard or the house—she was great there, and her strength was only a boon. Not for her friends. Aveline and Purcell were always happy to help her with her projects as she'd helped them with so many of theirs. For Fallon.

It couldn't have been more clear than the afternoon Fallon had elected to spend as a picker to clear her head about a fiddly rebuild.

Aveline and Purcell were resting in a spot of shade. Their coveralls were unzipped, hanging from their waists. Reflected sunlight gleamed rich red-golds off their exposed skin. Fallon didn't have the heart to warn them of skin cancer—children of the broken world, they knew the dangers same as everyone. Aveline was in a sports bra and cut-up t-shirt, Purcell just in his binder.

Keri was with them, of course, the sun shining just as warmly off her bronze-plated casing. She hadn't made herself taller, but she was solid now in ways she'd never been before. Her case no longer tried to mimic a human look. There were decorative seams across her arms and shoulders, bolts exposed down her back. The android's thin white tank top stretched tight over her powerful chest. She'd done something with her casing so it flexed with the moving of her hydraulics. Keri was nothing that wanted to look human, and she was beautiful.

And she was Fallon's employee. Fallon kept her hands to herself, even if she couldn't always keep her eyes or thoughts off the android.

Purcell waved when he spotted Fallon, and Keri turned to smile at her in greeting. She still had the same face, but it communicated so differently with the bolder body language of her power behind it. Keri had looked like a sweet waif before, someone to protect; now she was capable and confident—displayed strength Fallon could all too easily imagine melting against. Keri couldn't have been better designed to test Fallon's control if she'd tried.

"Anything you need us for, Fallon?" Keri asked when she joined them in the shade.

"Just company, if you don't mind," Fallon answered. "Thought I'd do some picking, for old times' sake."

The pickers made her welcome, and chose a target to strip to the bones. It was meditative to wield a demag and a screwdriver and fill boxes with dials and wires and resistors and gears and control boards and all the little components you'd never know were in even a small transport from the outside. Getting the hover drives and mag thrusters off was more tricky, but it was the kind of work Fallon had been doing since she was a kid. Keri stripped the paneling off, rolling it onto tubes with her fingers denting the metal into place. Fallon swallowed hard as she watched the flex of the android's arms, and then turned her gaze quickly back to the hover drive she was working on. She only hoped that the heat of her face would be attributed to the warmth of the day.

With the transport stripped, Purcell wanted to catalog the newest shipment. There were sometimes good finds—duffel bags of clothes, or books; things that weren't supposed to go to the Junkyard but came in anyway. There were a few big transport buses and smaller vehicles stacked up with crates of electronics. The pile looked stable. It should have been stable. Fallon hung behind while Purcell ran ahead with all the energy of youth to begin exploring.

He'd hardly climbed his way in when everything began to shift with a sickening grind of metal.

"Purcell! Get out!" Fallon screamed. Aveline tried to run to Purcell, but Fallon grabbed her and dragged her back to safety. Aveline struggled, but Fallon couldn't let her die in the meat-grinder that was taking Purcell.

If Keri hadn't been there, the most brilliant builder the Junkyard had ever seen would have died. The android threw herself into the pile, punching through the paneling on a bus to grab its frame. The hydraulics across her back and arms strained through her coveralls as she planted herself and shoved against the direction of shift. Everything steadied just long enough for Purcell to crawl out and run to Fallon, whites showing all around his eyes.

Keri gave one last shove against the stack with all the power in her compact body. The bus rocked back, giving her time to run. Broken machinery crashed down behind her as the stack slumped over with the scream of metal and crash of glass.

Fallon's hands shook as she patted Purcell down, checking that he was unharmed. Aveline pushed her aside to cling to him, and Fallon turned to the android. Her hands were stroking all over Keri's body, checking everything she could feel through her casing before her mind caught up.

"Are you hurt? You didn't damage anything?" she asked. The android flexed, hydraulics tensing and releasing in a wave down her body.

"I'm fine." Keri smiled up at Fallon, resting a smooth metal hand over hers, and she remembered this was her employee she was groping. She dropped her hands like Keri's coveralls had burned her and turned back to the still-settling pile.

"Who did this?" she growled through bared teeth. "Whatever supplier delivered me a shoddy stack is never getting another order from me! People could have died!"

People did *not* die while working at the Junkyard. It was unacceptable. Fallon began the long march back to the front office, fists clenched, to give a royal telling off to whoever had nearly killed Purcell.

The anger was not enough to distract her from the feel of Keri's powerful hydraulics flexing beneath her hands, the delicate touch of fingers that could tear the paneling off a transport without a thought.

Keri was ruthless, pulling and teasing at Fallon's nipples until her tits ached with pleasure and her sex was slick with want where she ground it against the android's smoothly flexing body.

Fallon could only answer with a wordless denial, nearly a wail, when Keri pushed her leg down to make her stand on her own two feet again. Her throat was past the point of making coherent words. Keri's hands slid around Fallon's bare waist and pushed both boxers and coveralls down to the floor. Fallon managed, somehow, to kick her shaking legs free of them so she stood in only her boots.

"Beautiful," Keri declared, and Fallon stole a kiss from her sweet lips before Keri's strong hands wrapped around Fallon's hips to pick her up as though she weighed nothing. Which she did, to the android. She was light as featherdown to Keri and made an undignified squawk as she was lifted. Keri easily settled Fallon's legs over her broad shoulders, hands supporting Fallon's back. Fallon's shoulders were still resting against the wall of the work shed, just higher up now.

Keri grinned at her from between her legs, and Fallon's breath caught in her throat before the android even leaned forward to capture her clit between smooth bronze lips.

If Keri hadn't been holding her so securely, Fallon could have squirmed her way clear off her shoulders. The sorted components in their boxes shifted and rustled on their shelves as Fallon bucked under Keri's too-clever ministration. Cool lips sucked and kissed her clit, and Keri's tongue flicked circles faster and lighter than thought. Fallon all but sobbed with the intensity of the pleasure as it grew hot and tight up the arching column of her spine.

It was so good, so much better than she'd even dared dream when she fantasized in the privacy of her bedroom—and then Keri's tongue grew impossibly long. It was still rubbing against her clit while it slid into Fallon and curved up just right to vibrate inside her.

Fallon climaxed with her fingers digging into the android's wiry hair and Keri's name screaming out of her throat.

"I quit."

Fallon looked up at the unexpected words, at Keri stripped of her coveralls so she stood in tight jeans and a tiny halter top that did nothing to conceal the way her hydraulics flexed under her bronze casing. She shoved her carefully folded coveralls at Fallon, who accepted them in shock.

"I..." Fallon started, before she bit back all her arguments. No one owed her anything. This wasn't the first pair of coveralls she'd gotten back on a Friday night after the pay was handed out.

"Thank you," Fallon said, looking down at her grease-stained hands clenching tight on the worn fabric of the coveralls. "It's been good having you. I'm sure you'll do well wherever you go."

There. Polite words said. People came and went all the time. Didn't matter if this person was the one Fallon's eyes could never stop watching, the one she pictured when she was having a private moment with her vibe. Maybe it was even Fallon's scrutiny that had driven Keri away. She'd tried not to be inappropriate, but she knew the android had caught her looking more than once.

"You're welcome in the house as long as you need to stay, of course," Fallon said, backing up to go put the coveralls away. Maybe if she mixed them in with all the others she'd never know which had been Keri's and it wouldn't haunt her to see them on someone else.

"I don't work for you anymore," Keri said, following her.

"Yes, that's what quitting means," Fallon agreed. "Do you have something lined up? I'll give you a good reference, if you need it." She was a good boss. The Junkyard was a good place to work for everyone, even if her heart was breaking for losing what she'd never had in the first place. She gently placed Keri's coveralls on the top of the neatly folded stack in the "smalls" box.

"Is there anything else you need?" Fallon asked the android, who was still following her. Everyone else was gone now; it was just the two of them.

"I don't work for you. What's stopping you from kissing me *now?*" Keri asked.

"I...." Fallon took a step back.

"Because I was a companion for a very long time. I can tell when someone wants me," Keri talked over Fallon's half-formed objections. "You want me so bad it burns under your skin, but you won't do anything but look. I was your employee—I wouldn't have minded; I wanted you from the first time I saw you—but I understand. Now, I don't work for you. Is there any reason you won't have me?"

"Keri..." Fallon tried, but it came out of her throat as a hungry whimper and she had no words to follow it with. Not with the android staring her down, stepping closer with the hydraulics flexing under her gleaming bronze casing, all confidence and strength.

"I think...." Keri's voice was quieter, a smile playing on her lips. "Maybe the boss-lady needs someone else to take charge for a little bit?" She was so close now. One hand reached up to rest whisper-gentle on the back of Fallon's neck, crushing power perfectly controlled, and Fallon's entire body shuddered.

"Please," Fallon breathed. Keri's chromed teeth flashed in the briefest of smiles as she pulled Fallon down to kiss her deep. Fallon groaned against cool bronze lips, her hands stroking across the overwhelming power of the android's back and shoulders as Keri's explored her in turn. One of Keri's palms came to rest in the center of Fallon's chest, and she broke the kiss to smile, bright and hungry. She shoved Fallon back with perfectly calibrated strength.

Fallon's shoulders hit the wall of the work shed hard enough to make the little components sorted in their boxes jump on the shelves.

"God, yes," she moaned.

"Wow," Fallon said, which seemed to be the current limit of her eloquence. Keri had safely lowered her to the floor, placing her on her discarded coveralls to keep her off the dirty concrete. Fallon slumped over to rest her shoulder against the android sitting companionably beside her. Her entire body felt warm and limp, like an overboiled noodle, and she giggled at the thought. Keri wrapped one powerful arm around Fallon's back, and she nuzzled against the android's bronze casing.

She'd wanted this so badly... and that thought sobered her. The only reason she'd gotten to have this was because Keri was leaving. She'd quit. This had been a goodbye fuck, or something like it.

Fallon quickly blinked the tears from her eyes. She gently

stroked Keri's shoulder, feeling the hydraulics, the seams in her plated casing.

"I'll miss you," she said quietly. It was always hard to lose one of the core at the Junkyard or the house.

"Mmm, I'm out of a job." Keri's smooth hand stroked Fallon's back. "I heard about a great place to work. A woman who watched the breaking of the world and let the sorrow of it make her *kind*. She built herself a tiny empire, a chosen family of strays, with her arms wide open to welcome anyone in. Fallon in her Junkyard, grease-stained angel of hope in a sea of despair. Do you think she'd give a broken-down old companion android a job? I wouldn't want to work anywhere else."

"Keri...." Fallon could feel herself blushing at the description. She wasn't all that. "If you were working for me, we couldn't...." She bit her tongue. Why should she assume Keri wanted to have more than just this once together?

"Nah." Keri laughed. "We have a preexisting relationship now. Giving your lover a job isn't harassing your employees, it's just nepotism."

Fallon laughed with her. Keri wanted her, wanted to be in the Junkyard and in her arms. The knowledge settled like a bubble of golden light in Fallon's chest.

"You've thought of everything, haven't you?" she accused, and Keri nodded with a smile on her sweet face.

"Kiss me?" Fallon asked, laughing again as she was picked up and deposited in the android's lap for it. Keri stroked her bare back, the hydraulics in her neck and shoulders shifting beneath Fallon's hands. Her lips were cool and smooth and tasted of solder smoke and the tang of Fallon's own musk.

Nothing in the world could be more perfect.

LIGHTNING THEN, AND MOTION

ERIC DEL CARLO

Fingers slid into the waistband of my greasy trousers, hooked firmly, then started tugging, down over the modest, taut swells of my ass. I grinned, wedged halfway under my junk-bucket rig, and did nothing to stop whoever it was. Didn't have time. My work torch hummed white light onto my busy hands. Tools rang musically as I picked up one, then the next. Had to work fast. The Depravity, whatever it was, was going to reach some kind of crescendo tonight. It might fizz out after that. I was damned sure going to fly my illegal-as-hell rig into it before it vanished out of the high lavender sky of this world.

Meanwhile, somebody was shucking my pants down to my knees, exposing my bare butt to the evening air. I had my weight on my elbows. Every instrument I needed to have a chance at flightworthiness lay within my reach.

Lube-y fingers slipped between the halves of my ass, and grazed my hole. I heard a mutter of pleasure from beyond the small, crude bulk of my vessel.

There were dozens of us out on the orange desert floor tonight, maybe hundreds. Rigs of every fabrication and level of functionality. That was a lot of mechanized rebellion. We never would have massed like this, not if the Depravity, a white god's-eye unblinking upon the night, hadn't brought its mysterious coruscating energies to this imminent zenith after a year of hanging in our sky. It felt like a last chance, a once-in-a-lifetime opportunity that, if we let it go by, we'd relive as aching, bitter fantasies for the rest of our time.

I couldn't miss it. I wouldn't.

Because, of course, it wasn't just about the enigmatic, awesome phenomenon that had appeared above our backwater colony worldlet. The spectacle had attracted endless scientific interest, but nobody cared anything about us, the natives, the luckless ones who worked in mines and fields and labs and somehow never saw the yield of our efforts.

Authorities still measured things in Earthyears, and I'd lived enough of those to be tried as an adult for whatever I did from here on out. You found trouble on a world like this, or else you created it, just to give the bleak landscape of your existence some aesthetic nuance.

Tonight, though, would be the do or die event. I thrummed like any of the exposed live couplings on my rig's undercarriage, ones that could electrocute me instantly. I labored to give maximum power to my little craft.

A slick fingertip worked itself into my asshole. Reflexive pleasures radiated their tendrils through my body. I heard the jingling of buckles, along with the growing growls of desire. I finally gathered enough of the sounds to know it was Sampson back there. But I really didn't have time for him.

So when I felt him shifting, putting himself into position, I just kept on working. Sampson was a parts guy. Many parts people inhabited the riggers scene, for obvious reasons. We needed their bibs and bobs, their salvage. Sampson and I had been now-and-again lovers, and tonight, evidently, he couldn't let me go without a last screw. I was okay with that. I just couldn't really participate in it.

Even so, when his thick lubed cock pressed to my hole and started sliding its way in, my own cock swelled. About half the time I can come from a dude fucking my ass, even without touching myself. Tonight I couldn't spare either the concentration or a free hand to get myself off. Sampson grunted, "Kolpek! This sweet hole! Fuck...." Other such endearments followed, as his pace sped.

I wouldn't have minded if he'd approached me a week ago, or two nights ago, or last night, even. We could have made love properly. I'd had more than a few farewell screws recently, men and women who had meant something to me, and ones who'd just been fun. Several among those had been fellow riggers, who would be lifting for the high sky tonight alongside me.

Nobody knew how many of us would back out at the last second, how many would be taken down by the policers. Or how many would die in the attempt to reach the Depravity.

"Kolpek!" Sampson shouted my name again, and this time his liquid love erupted deep inside me. My cock gave a twitch, but I was too remote from orgasm to share in his. I was finishing up the last of the connections, juicing my salvage-parts bird with the final spurts of power I could offer it.

Sampson pulled himself out of me. At any point I could have told him to knock it the fuck off, and he would have gone away. He wiped the backs of my thighs with a cloth. I turned off my glaring work torch and wriggled out from underneath my rig. The settling night blew soft against my face as I did up my trousers. Nearby clangs and curses and laughter told me of riggers' camaraderie, of shared purpose and intent. Probably a lot of other last-minute screws were going on, on the pilot seats, bodies pressed standing against gritty outer hulls, or grappling on the ground for all to see—because why not? We were a fast, loose community, uninhibited, reckless.

Before I turned to Sampson, I looked out over the desert. It was a rock of a world. Beautiful in its way. Or it would have been if most of the people colonizing it weren't shackled to lives made deliberately hopeless by government, by corporate interests, by evil-ass greed.

But we improvised. We played a game behind the game. Official personal transports were for our world's small but vicious aristocracy. Yet riggers had sprung into existence explicitly because of those restrictions. We had made do. We were trained for work with machinery, and we had adapted those talents. Again, a big fuck you.

I looked for Havad among the rigs laid out across the open desert. I sought the shape of her craft, the high dorsal-like fin, but couldn't find it among the hulks, lit by sparks, by arc flares. I looked for Havad herself, a pointless task in the assembled gloom. I found her image anyway, playing against a back wall of my brain, a surface left somehow untouched by everything else in my life, my disappointments, my frustrations, the driving need to rebel against any motherfucker I perceived as having control over my destiny.

Havad was out here tonight. I was certain. I felt I could breathe in her chill scent. If I reached out a hand, I would brush the stiff tips of her shorn hair. If I called her name, even whispered it, she would hear. But would she answer? I didn't know that.

She was a fellow rigger. One of the elite. I could judge Havad's talents because I was an elite rigger too. I did not feel her to be my rival. Rather... my match, my mate. And yet I had never been able to speak more than a dozen words to her, and had rarely met her blue eyes.

And yet and yet....

All that nonsense and I believed I really loved her. Or would love her, given the guts and opportunity to present myself. I was an adult, according to my world's authorities, but where lovely, able Havad was concerned, I was a dumbstruck boy.

Finally I turned to Sampson. He was a big man with a long face which tonight stretched mournfully. His permanently greased hands bunched at his sides, and I wondered for the first time if he thought of me as something more than a fun lay, if I had a special significance in his mind, his heart. Again, it was something he should have come to me sooner with. Well, at least he'd had me one last time. It was more than I'd ever managed with Havad.

"You really going up?" His eyes, also sorrowful tonight, flicked upward.

I felt the Depravity burning above. It was visible everywhere in this hemisphere, defying logic and all proper analysis. A popular non-scientific theory was that aliens had put the thing into the sky of our little world. Amusing. Two centuries of exploration and colonization, and humankind had not encountered any life which could fittingly be called an alien species. If we do, I hope we come up with a less demeaning word than "alien."

Sampson's eyes came back down, and I met them. Others must have been asking that same question, over and over, on this desert tonight. *You really going up?* We riggers had dedicated ourselves to this wild undertaking, a great mass delusion, a quest. We wouldn't all succeed. Most of us wouldn't. Actually, maybe none of us at all. It was the ultimate fool's errand, after all.

I said, "Fuck yeah, I'm going up."

It was a glorious, howling madness, a cascade of noise and danger. My rig rocked and rattled. The instrument bar was lit bright, pulsing with every particle of strength I could coax from the slapped-together engine.

Now we were up, yowling through the night. I had never been off the ground with so many others. This felt like exodus, like some great historical improbable escape. A hundred clattering ships, spewing sparks, venting exhaust. Blazing across the sky, climbing, climbing.

I had no thought of family, of lovers left behind. Certainly I expended no mental energy on my colorless life on this rock, the might-as-well-be-a-slave job I'd been assigned. Only rigging had awakened my passion, given me something to believe in.

This, then, was the ultimate expression of that belief. Dissent writ large, tearing up the nighttime, criminal vessels all aiming for the highest point, the peak of the lavender sky.

My controls shuddered under my hands. My leather coat creaked on my thin frame. I had tied back my long, dark hair earlier. Now it came free, and sweaty strands striped my forehead, fell across my cheeks. I grinned wickedly. I was gaining altitude, along with most of the others. A few craft here and there in this mad herd were failing, dropping back to the ground. I didn't worry about those riggers; they had tried, and if they survived their landings, they would forever be able to say they had participated in this lunatic glory of shrieking engines.

Above, still above, the Depravity whirled and crackled. The desert was far below now. Its energies remained baffling, its purpose enigmatic, if indeed the spectacle could be said to have a purpose. That implied some intelligence behind the Depravity, and nobody of any scientific credibility was willing to commit to that romantic possibility.

My canopy was radiant with the strange light. The air was growing chill, fingers of true cold working beneath my coat now. Riggers didn't fly this high. The lofty altitude was going to knock out a few more engines, maybe mine among them. I merely grinned more fiercely and pushed my clanking tub harder and higher.

New light suddenly splashed across the cloudless ether. New mechanized shapes appeared, rising around us, among us. The policers. Of course. Our mass migration had been detected, or else, with so big an undertaking and so many people aware of it ahead of time, somebody had squealed to the authorities.

I didn't care. I hammered upward.

Shiny craft with official markings, with angry lights spinning, came to tyrannize us. Their voices rang out among the cacophony of laboring engines. We were told we were criminals. We were ordered to return to the surface, immediately. Consequences were mentioned. I still didn't care.

A sleek policer unit reared off my starboard. I lifted a middle finger and pressed it to my canopy.

I felt above it all. I felt free. These might be the last feelings I ever had, and I was ready to go out this way, if it came to that.

The marvel of the Depravity loomed hugely, and that seemed to have happened all of a sudden, even though we had been approaching it at a steady, measurable pace. I had seen pictures, of course. Study craft had been up here. Unpersoned probes, supposedly, had even been launched into the swirling sphere of unknown energy.

The Depravity filled my cockpit now, poured its fantastic light onto me, into every pore of my flesh, saturating me to my bones. I was aiming right at the heart. Only now did I realize how few craft still accompanied me. So many had fallen off. The policer units were firing nets and lacing the dark below with frightening yellow traceries. They didn't want anybody interfering with their precious Singularity or Entanglement or whatever the hell they would eventually decide to officially call it.

But I knew the truth. It didn't belong to them. The Depravity was a gift for the improvisers, for those of us who could truly wing it.

The fringe of the thing was snapping and swirling toward the skin of my rig. It had an interior, I saw, or thought I saw in those frantic instants. Crazy landscapes roiled and billowed, seas of foaming electricity crashing and heaving. It was massive. And it seemed to me, the clear thought sounding behind my adrenalized grin and the roar of overtaxed mechanization, that this Depravity had indeed changed in its steady nature, that it was coming to some unguessable finale. It did in truth possess a purpose, and my effort had been timed precisely. I was arriving at the chosen moment.

The thought, that last bit of my own thinking, pleased me.

Then I was truly inside the thing.

Then there came lightning, a titanic burst of it, made up of psychotic colors and formidable strength.

Lightning. Then—

When the vast surging motion ended, I thought the universe would break apart. I expected some terrible repercussion, an inertial revenge. I felt I had traveled fast, far too fast, beyond the bounds of any rational physics.

But there was only a bump, a soft thump, and then stillness. All that forward motion I'd experienced ceased.

My canopy was a smear of gray and black. My instrument bar slept, and when I prodded it, it didn't awaken. The high-altitude cold had gone. My rig was silent. My heartbeat was a lonesome sound adrift on my ringing eardrums.

I moved as if softened by a hangover, with muscles unhurt but slightly flaccid. Manual catches came undone with more effort than I normally had to use. A hatch fell away.

I stepped out into a gentle, steady, consuming brilliance.

There was no glare to hold my hand up against, no source of radiance to block out. The glow was everywhere. I squinted, though the light didn't hurt. My first impressions: I stood on ground, there was sky above, with landscape of some kind surrounding. These basic, familiar standards comforted me, although I did not feel panic.

Patting my body, my limbs, I assured myself I was all here, and wondered why I'd imagined I might not be. I already knew I hadn't been injured. That had been no crash I'd experienced; it was a landing. I had arrived. Where?

The luminescence relented somewhat, or more likely I adjusted to it. The ground was a soft grit, finely grained but more than firm enough for easy walking, as I learned with a few experimental steps. The sky was milky in color with gradations that suggested climate. The land beneath stretched in all directions, as land is apt to. I saw outcroppings, randomly placed, a natural terrain. Distant skeletal shapes might have been trees, might have been leaning monuments.

I felt an ease here. I didn't question it, not yet.

My rig had suffered in the journey. Its hull was crumpled, though not catastrophically. The smeared gray and black on the canopy coated the whole surface. It looked like a residue, something viscous. I went to a knee and looked underneath at the engine. I didn't need to examine it. It was through.

What was I supposed to do here? There seemed, strangely, no urgency to that question. I turned my back on my rig and began to walk. The motion renewed strength in my limbs. The limpness gradually left me. I started to feel a growing eagerness, though the excitement had no focus, no direction. Suddenly I thought of Sampson, and wished I had paid more attention when he had fucked me earlier. That instance seemed now precious for some reason, and I would have liked to have truly been in that moment, feeling his penetration, meeting his pleasure with some of my own. Phantom memories of his cock inside my ass. I should have gone along with that, should have let my natural arousal overtake me. I should have come, right along with Sampson, the big, sentimental mechanic.

I knew I would never see him again.

I closed on an object nearer than any of those distant leaning structures. This too was canted at an angle. I blinked, then recognized the dorsal fin. My breath went short, and I ran toward the craft. I came up to the rig, coated like mine in a syrupy soot.

Havad wasn't inside. I breathed hard, fantastically relieved not to have found her limp, sprawled body. I stepped back. A new determination awoke in me. I found footprints marking the grit and told myself they could only be hers. I set out at a jog, then ran again, eager to find her.

As I pounded across the land, aiming toward one of the skeletal columns, more phantom remembrances assailed me. Sampson. Tuvec. Ho-Klum. Many others. Faces and hands and mouths and orifices. I was awash in my sexual past, as if the memories were being shocked out of their mental caches with electrical prods.

Sweat streamed beneath my leather coat. My lean body ached with desire. The landscape started to blur as heat filled my skull.

Where the fuck was I? How the hell had I gotten here? Finally, those crucial questions exploded across my mind. I remembered the seconds when the Depravity had consumed my rig. That monstrous, inexplicable thing had... eaten me? And this was what lay inside? Or had it transported me to some strange realm?

Despite my profound need to know, I ran on with the same determination, with the same objective in mind: find Havad.

But as I raced, footsteps thumping and heart hammering, I saw flashes at the periphery of my smeary vision. They were mere hard flashes of almost-color, things standing against the milky sky and sallow terrain. Upright things. Shelled, perhaps. Beetle-like. Turquoise. Aquamarine. But not there when I turned for a look; just vanishing. Mirages.

I approached a stand of trees.

They were indeed skeletal, like a clutch of bones all bound together, quite tall. Some kind of coppery foliage decorated their tops. Below this little cluster of bone trees was a pool, and the liquid contained there was as milky as the sky. Yet it looked rich, soothing, immensely cool. I was steaming with sweat. My slim muscles ached.

A shape, previously submerged, came up out of that milk-water. I stood panting on the brink and watched the body unfold upward, limbs strong and sleek, skin glistening. Her breasts were high and firm. Whitish globules glimmered in her cropped hair. She heaved in a breath, as though she'd been under a while.

I was standing near where she had left her clothing.

Peripherally, the brim of the oasis flickered with the bluish beetle-shapes, but they weren't really there, not in any way that mattered, not so they could interfere or intrude upon us.

Havad wiped her eyes and looked up at me.

"It's Kolpek," I told her, thinking she might not even know my name.

She studied me a moment, with the milk drizzling from her, all the lovely curves and lengths of her. Finally she said, "Of course it is. Who else would make it through?"

She knew me. Naturally, she knew me. It was stupid to imagine she wouldn't. We were riggers, among the best of that class of makeshift daredevils.

Her body's pigment was richer than mine, deeper, her eyes a penetrating blue. The cropped plumage of her hair looked as hard and bright as ivory. I desired her. And I loved her, wanted to love her, hoped to prove my love was better than infatuation, than boyish obsession.

"*What* did we make it through?" I asked.

She lifted her lovely, molded shoulders. "The Depravity. The Singularity. The... whatever. It brought us here. I have the feeling it's gone now, closed behind us."

I realized I'd had that feeling too, beating just below my immediate thoughts. I could see the whirling, fiery crackle shrinking rapidly in on itself above my former world. Collapsing. Disappearing. Disappointing all those cautious scientific minds.

"So we're stranded here," I said.

"Does that sound so bad?"

I hadn't said it like it was. "No." A grin tugged at my lips, and I let it show.

Havad gazed a moment more at me, steadily, blue eyes searching, a hunger beginning to show in them. She said, "Come into the water with me."

I wanted the cool kiss of that water. I needed it, after my run. I dropped the coat off my shoulders, undid my greasy trousers. Her eyes stayed on me. I stepped naked to the pool's edge, where the sand darkened. I couldn't see the bottom through the cloudy liquid, but Havad was standing, thigh-deep. I slipped down into the water.

It was cool but not bracingly so. It washed the sweat from me, and seemed to touch my flesh with a curious charge. Tingling impulses raced over me, minute, invisible sparks. I dunked myself all the way under and was suffused with that strange energy.

I came up gasping. I raked the long, wet hanks of my hair off my face and found Havad smiling at me. I wasn't sure I had ever seen her smile before. She had always been such a focused rigger, fine-tuning her bird, inducing it to greater speeds. She, I believed, had always understood what our movement was truly about. She grasped the rebellion, was eager to fuck up the works of the system which had effectively enslaved our world.

It was a beautiful smile, a soft, knowing spread of lips. It included her eyes, widening the blue orbs slightly, shining a personal light on me. I stood facing her. Her body gleamed.

"Havad..." I started to say, wanting to truly present myself, to make my argument for the worthiness of my love for her.

But she didn't want to hear what I had to say. Not now anyway. She took a sloshing step toward me, pulled me into her strong arms, and laid her mouth hard against me, tipping her head to the side and mashing her lips on mine. The contact was as electric as the stimulating milk bath we stood in—more so. It shot a hot force through me, a sweet heat which entered my cells. The desire I'd felt up until now was nothing, a pantomime, a promise of passion to come. Now it was here, on me, inside me. I wanted this woman beyond all rationality.

I closed my arms tightly around her, and drove my mouth onto hers, answering the kiss. Our lips parted; tongues entangled. I had stood near enough to her in the past to have caught her strangely cool scent, a chilled aura tipped with lively musk. Even soaked as she was, that fragrance filled me now. I breathed her in as I tasted her, my tongue alive on hers.

My suddenly hardened cock caught between our pressing bodies. I shifted, laid my length against her rigid lower belly. Her breasts pushed against me. I held her waist. She gripped my bony shoulders.

As we kissed, I felt at some remote level of perceptibility the pressure of attention. Eyes. But not quite eyes. I felt... watched. But as it had been when I'd made my suicidal attempt at reaching the Depravity, I didn't care about anything but my immediate goal. All else was distant interference, static. I wanted only Havad.

We writhed against each other now, our full physical selves coming to life and participating in this joining. I staggered a step on the silty pool bottom, held onto her slick, taut body. I lifted a hand to her breast and squeezed. She dropped a palm onto my ass and gripped the flesh there. It was all happy, all joyous. I had never quite let myself imagine carnal relations with this person, but no fantasy could have spoiled this reality.

Her breath was hot on my collarbone as she nuzzled me. Her nipple stiffened between my fingers. I coaxed the bud, then lowered my mouth to it. When I flicked her with my tongue, she arched her back, making a bow of herself.

She reached between us, and her fingers lightly encircled my straining shaft. They were good, talented fingers. They plucked the bulge of my underside vein. Her thumb smeared my sensitive crown, arousing a wriggle of delight in me. She laughed, a soft pant of gaiety. If I hadn't seen her smile before, then I'd surely never heard that laugh. She had been such a dedicated rigger, practically grim about the cause.

But now I held her and kissed her, and she was a living, joyful, sexual being. I sucked ardently at her other nipple. She cupped my balls and nibbled on my earlobe. I groped her flank, the tight curve of her thigh where it disappeared into the water.

Finally I had to feel her sex. I slid my hand along the inner curvature of her thigh, lifted my fingertips. She trembled and anchored her fingers into the thin meat of my back. My knuckles brushed damp curls, then I felt the first heat and intimate moisture of her. Her lips were slippery. Her back flexed again when I made my first ingress, and her body rolled against me.

I waited an instant, until she planted a small, meaningful kiss on my throat; then I pressed further up into her, using two fingers. Silken flesh closed around my middle knuckles. I felt the fibrous play of animate tissue within her. She squeezed and twined, and all the softness inside didn't disguise the hard need of her body. She ground herself on my fingers, finding a stance and digging that anchoring hand harder into my back. She rode my digits and didn't now kiss my throat; instead, she bit, and the pain was thrilling.

Havad shook and jerked, and tightened herself deliciously on my fingers.

She looked up at me, and a grin notched her comely face for the first time, a wicked leer. She reached for me again, hunkering slightly, slipping her hand between my legs, past my balls. When her fingertips grazed my butthole, I jumped. She waited to see what the response meant. I gave her a reciprocating grin.

The first digit entered my puckered hole. This time it wasn't the semi-indifferent penetration it had been with Sampson. I was fully aware of the spreading pleasure, the slow threads of rapture. Havad took her time, sliding her finger up into me. I felt the swell of her knuckle. I brushed my lips against her temple, feeling the stiff tufts of her ivory hair. A narrow vein beat there, excited blood pumping.

When she eeled a second finger inside, I gasped. The intimacy was exquisite. My cock throbbed against her lower abdomen, drizzling a fluid as milky as this strange water we wallowed in.

As she had done, I ground down on the intrusions, forcing her fingers deeper. New pleasures opened up within me with every inch. My channel squeezed her tightly, but she kept up the incursion, twisting the fingers, corkscrewing her way, fingering my ass with fervor.

Had she kept it up, I would have come that way, spraying spunk up between us, gluing our writhing bodies together with my seed. But she wanted something else, and I was overjoyed to accommodate her.

She withdrew her fingers and moved half a step back, eyeing me like she was gauging a slope she meant to climb. Then with a nimble move she vaulted up into my arms, circling my waist with her legs, arms crossed behind my neck. She lowered herself with delirious insistence onto my rampant cock.

I planted my stance and cradled her, forearms under her thighs, palms cupping her ass. Her dripping pussy sheathed my staff. Our pelvic bones came together. I carried her full weight. We shifted a bit, found the right balance. Then she proceeded to buck atop me, lifting and dropping.

She was lovely and lithe. Her arms were hard bars across my shoulders. Her thighs and calves squeezed me. I helped with the tempo she set, clutching that bouncing ass. Her face rocked back and forth before mine, eyelids fluttering over a shade of piercing blue. Her mouth was open, breaths shortening.

I felt the deep heat of her. She slammed herself down onto my cock, again and again. Her breasts jounced. A deep boil of pleasure started in my balls. My flesh burned with a rising bliss. The water splashed against my straining legs. Overhead, the white sky wheeled. Havad was crying out. So was I, inarticulate sounds, carnal translations of the words I wanted to say to her. But maybe I didn't need to argue my love. Maybe this was enough.

She rode and writhed and wriggled, and when she clenched herself hard around me and sobbed out a crescendo, I lost every bit of control. The eruption felt huge. I jetted up into her. It was like being turned inside out. No—it was like going up into the Depravity, into its roiling interior. It was lightning and motion, all at once.

After that fantastic climax, and as the first ebbings took my body into a sweet aching embrace, Havad unlocked her cinching legs. I let her down into the water.

We smiled at one another, in a shy but pleasant way.

We kissed.

She took my hand, and we went to the shore of the oasis. When we lay down on the damp sand, on our backs, side by side, I looked up and saw fruit of some sort hanging in the lower branches of the bone trees. They were a lighter copper shade than the high foliage, oval and textured. I wondered if they were edible, then thought for no real reason that they must be.

Near where we lay I noticed a smaller pool, the water in it clear and sparkling. Drinking water, surely.

Finally, raising languid eyes I saw the human-sized upright beetle-shapes who had come to watch us. I heard a faint chittering, as if they were excitedly discussing what they'd seen. They still weren't entirely tuned into this dimension, it seemed; or else they were semi-cloaked for protective reasons. Answers, I guessed, would be forthcoming. Obviously they wanted us here. Maybe not *us* specifically, but Havad and I were the ones who had braved the Depravity and made it through.

Whatever they were, I would not refer to them as aliens.

She nestled against me, and I laid an arm over her. She kissed my throat gently, and I felt the rightness of everything. My mate and I, stranded in paradise.

THE FORGE
KELLY ROSE PFLUG-BACK

At the first light of dawn I wake from dreams of Raphael, her hair falling around my face like dark feathers. Dew has left a cold sheen on my face and on the outside of my sleeping bag, the branches above me thick with the gravelly voices of ravens, calling to each other through the morning's frigid air. The trunks of the spruce trees sigh in the wind, and I can feel the platform beneath me swaying—a feeling that terrified me for my first few weeks at the camp, and still sometimes does.

I undo the buckles of the nylon hip harness that secures me to the tree with a rappel line, pushing my hands under my pants and thermal tights, closing my eyes against the brightening sun. In my head she's straddling my face with her thick, perfect thighs as my tongue works at her swollen clit, engorging it with blood, her hips moving snake-like while she moans and moans. In my head she's kneeling between my thighs, her dark eyes heavy-lidded as she watches herself fuck me. My hips are bucking against my hand now, and I come thinking about those eyes, the liquid-dark of them, somehow the sexiest part of her. So disarming I can't stand to hold her gaze for more than a second or else I'm scared she'll see me shudder, see the way she gets under my skin without even trying.

It occurs to me often how much time I waste just thinking about what her hands would feel like all over my body. Guilt nags at my conscience as I strap my dull climbing spurs onto my boots and rappel down the forty-something feet of redwood between my platform and the ground. I can already hear the voices of the others, laughing over oatmeal and cowboy coffee at the morning fire. Their faces turn to me as I pad down the loamy earth toward the clearing, and Dylan is the first to chastise.

"Sleeping in again, Meghan! The revolution will not be a tea party," he jokes in his thick Newfoundland accent, paraphrasing Marx, or Mao, or some other dead theorist I probably read about in undergrad and have long since forgotten. His taped-together glasses sit askew on his face, his hair sticking up at every angle. Even for someone who lives in the woods Dylan looks disheveled, but we forgive him his eccentricities because of his brilliance.

"Lay off, she was probably up late working on her thesis," Lurch teases, between shoveling spoonfuls of oatmeal into his mouth from a dented tin bowl. In the months that I've known him, the novelty that I live at the camp while writing a Master's thesis on the effects of deforestation on soil erosion doesn't seem to have worn off. Most of the other kids who frequent the camp are proud dropouts, career protesters who have too much disdain for the system to give it the satisfaction of their dependence. *By the time you graduate we're all going to be dead or living underground, anyway,* he always teases, and my heart sinks at the grain of truth in his pessimism. Faces tend to come and go as the months pass, but the five of us have stuck it out through the changing seasons, reinforcing the tarps during the winter's violent wind storms and blistering our hands raw building barricades on the logging roads.

The forest products companies do their endless dance with the team of environmental lawyers who come talk to us every week or so, sitting at the fire and trying to convince us that it just isn't worth it, the stakes are too high; people like us don't get processed through regular courts anymore, or sent to regular jails after they're sentenced. After nearly a year the judge still seems unconvinced of the legal viability of designating the forest as conservation land, despite my endless presentations on nematodes and nitrogen loss, sitting on the stand in my borrowed clothes, my fingernails still dark with crescents of dirt. Dylan has equipped the camp with radio scanners which he says will warn us of the military raid we're sure will happen any day now, give us a few minutes to scramble into our platforms and padlock ourselves to the trees. This will give us time to inform the press, cast a spotlight on the issue so that the authorities can't just disappear us in secret, bags over our heads and everything.

Mia makes room for me on the fallen log we use as fireside seating, and I squeeze in between her and Serje, who follows his usual routine of pretending I don't exist. I respond by following my own usual routine of pretending Mia's latest concoction of wild-gathered herbs is deeply interesting, feigning appreciation as I swill the bitter tinctures that she says will remove toxins from my liver, or stabilize my blood sugar, or prolong my unenviable life.

I go through the day in a haze, prickling with anxiety, dropping the hatchet while I'm splitting logs and losing my way twice on my way back from getting water from the spring. Raphael has come to the camp twice before, and said she would be here more if it weren't for the fact that the damp and the uneven ground make her bad leg hurt too much. Both times we stayed up for hours after everyone else had slunk off into the shadows, bleary-eyed with an exhaustion that her presence seemed to numb me to. It was me who thought of asking her for help, showing her the dull, rusted climbing spurs, explaining how we didn't have enough pairs for everyone and if the raids happened we would have to choose who stayed on the ground. Of course we'd discussed having more made at a metal shop in town, but the risks seemed too high. Unmarked cars with tinted windows and nondescript strangers in dark glasses seemed to stalk us whenever we left the camp, waiting to spot something indictable. Or, failing that, a moment when they could grab us with no witnesses.

After night falls I make my way through the underbrush that borders the logging roads with Serje and Dylan, leaving the others to keep watch for the few hours we'll be gone. The lights of a pickup truck slice wide corridors through the night, and we walk toward them with our eyes slitted like the nocturnal animals we've become. Rekha, Dylan's journalist friend from the city, steps out of the driver's seat dressed in a pair of jeans and an army jacket, carrying a tattered backpack which she's told me has accompanied her across five South American borders and survived one shipwreck.

"Meghan, you'd better still be up for an interview on soil analysis when you get back," she tells me, giving me a one-armed hug before tossing the keys to Dylan, which he immediately fumbles and drops. Her long hair brushes my face for a second, redolent with the scent of synthetic flowers, and it occurs to me that it's been weeks since I used shampoo.

"Of course," I tell her, climbing into the front seat beside Dylan as she disappears into the thicket that we just emerged from.

I let my mind wander as we drive through the darkness, listening to some 80s punk band Rekha left in the CD player. Dylan and Serje's voices just fade into the clanging music, all noise indistinguishable now to my bewildered mind.

We arrive on a lonely stretch of unpaved road on the outskirts of the city, where Dylan says it's best we park to avoid Raph being implicated in any way in case we're being watched. They start off into the woods in a straight line that will take us to the house and I hang back for a minute, leaning against the hood of the old truck, pulling the stub of a cigarette from my pocket, and flicking my dying lighter a few times. I don't hear Serje sneak up behind me, and he snatches the lighter out of my hand, laughing as he runs ahead into the trees.

I stand there for a second with my hand empty and my teeth gritted before picking up a crooked stick from the ground and holding it like an assault rifle, moving into the bracken all hunched over with my knees bent, avoiding dried-out deadfall that would snap under my feet and give away my presence.

I find him about twenty yards into the woods, tightrope-walking down a fallen tree trunk with his gangly arms held out, tattered hems of his sweater sleeves hanging down around his wrists, smoking a cigarette lit with my last precious Bic. I draw a bead on the back of his head and plot how best to ambush him, when something hits me in the side of my thigh, a dull thud stinging through the thick canvas of my overalls. I hear Dylan snicker in the bushes to my left, and Serje turns around too fast for me to hide, his eyes scanning the black thicket until they settle on me.

I throw the stick over my shoulder and rush him before he can react, taking him out at the legs and then pinning him down on the rocky ground, holding his arms with one knee and one hand while my other rifles through the pockets of his tattered, patched-up jeans. My hand closes around the lighter and I relax a bit, sitting down on his chest with all my weight while I light the nub of my smoke.

"I can't *breathe*, Meghan," he yells, and throws me off him before jumping to his feet. I just lie there and inhale the fruits of my long-suffering chase, throwing one arm behind my head, not caring if he decides to kick me. "I landed on a rock," he tells me, rubbing his elbow, dusting the forest's detritus from his pants and jacket. "You don't have to be so pissy just cause you get to see your girlfriend tonight." He pouts, and it strikes me why he probably stole my lighter in the first place.

Serje and I used to hook up back when I first got to the camp, always taking our sleeping bags and running off down the path together when everybody else was passing out besides the night watch. He told me he'd only been with two people before, and I loved the feeling of showing him stuff he'd never done. Blindfolding him with my bandanna and tying his hands behind his head, running the edge of my folding knife across his neck while I rode him; sliding my fingers into his ass while I kneeled in front of him with my mouth moving up and down his cock, rubbing his spot until his body tensed up and he came the way a girl comes, shaking and moaning, his muscles spasming while his come shot down my throat.

It wasn't that he was a bad lover. He'd spend what felt like hours just sucking on my clit, said he liked eating it so much he'd do it without wanting anything in return, yanking on my belt and pushing me down into the dirt when we were out scouting or repairing the trails together, groaning deep in the back of his throat so his tongue vibrated while he licked me, fucking me with one of his work-calloused hands while he pulled at his cock with the other.

But the longer our tryst went on the more I would find my mind wandering, thinking of other things no matter how good it was. He started wanting to sleep beside me at night, wanting to kiss me goodbye any time I went on a supply run back into the city.

When I started drooling over Raph I hadn't realized he'd be offended. Just off in my own selfish head, not even considering he could have been thinking this whole time that we were more than just friends.

"She's obviously not my girlfriend," I tell him, getting to my feet and taking one last haul off the smoke before I offer him kills. "I've hung out with her a grand total of twice. Doubt she even knows I exist," I say, and the words turn my stomach a bit with the fear that they're true.

"Whatever. You guys are totally gonna bang," he says, flicking away the cigarette's bent filter, and I feel a pang of remorse at the sadness underneath his snarky tone. I can't believe we're having this conversation now, getting emotional over a love triangle when one of the last old growth forests on the continent is at stake. I think about my research findings, the larger and larger patches of the earth that are now useless for growing crops, inhospitable to the species of plants and animals that once thrived here. If this downward spiral continues, soon only the wealthy will be able to afford non-synthetic food. The world is falling apart all around me, but my mind is somehow incapable of ranking its priorities, thoughts of her consuming me when I know I should be focused on more important things.

At the top of the hill, the lit-up squares of two tall, narrow windows wink at us through the trees. A small brick farmhouse, hidden in the woods at the end of a long, winding driveway. At its side, Raph's forge is built as an addition, converted from an old garage. Its big door is open for ventilation, even in the chill of late September, and as we depart from the tree line I can see the faint glow of her work lamps inside.

The others laugh and banter as we walk the stone footpath through Raph's overgrown garden, inhabited by its strange iron sculptures; prehistoric insects made of motorcycle parts, sea-monsters with jagged, rust-eaten spines. Dylan is passing around a flask of Mia's filthy-tasting homemade booze, the tartness of wild apples tinged with bitter devil's club—that bramble that makes the forest's valleys untraversable, which I would never have known was edible, let alone held medicinal properties, if it wasn't for her.

I can see Serje glancing at me from time to time from the corners of his eyes, reading my nervous posture, my hands that can't stop fiddling with the frayed cuffs of my sweater. Guilt rises up in my throat again, and I swallow it back down with another mouthful of the thick, bitter liquid, letting it loosen me with its warmth, calm the nerves which jangle more and more the closer we get to the house.

The heat of the forge hits us before we enter the open garage door. She stands surrounded by her work, hulking masses of metal bent and fused into monster silhouettes, the skeletons of strange and mythical beasts. A welding visor is pulled down over her face, and the long black tangles of her hair are tied back at the nape of her neck. She's wearing an old black sweatshirt, covered in holes from the sparks of the acetylene torch she holds, and a heavy leather apron.

"Hephaestus," Dylan calls, and she pulls up the visor of her mask and comes toward us, leaning on her wooden cane.

"Aphrodite," she jokes, taking his hand in her black-stained fingers and bowing as she kisses it, laughing in her raspy, deep voice, like velvet made from suede.

In the myths, Hephaestus is the one who forges weapons for the gods. He created Poseidon's trident and the armor that Achilles wore in the Trojan war. Just like Raph, he was born different, one of his legs withered from childhood, and his beautiful wife Aphrodite scorned him because of this.

The myths all describe Hephaestus as ugly, though, and no person could ever speak of Raph like that. Her dark eyes glitter when she turns her face to me, crooked smile flashing feline white teeth, and I feel the hairs on the back of my neck stand up. I can smell her sweat through the metallic air of the forge, and my mouth aches to taste her, to follow the beads of perspiration down her neck to the place where they pool between her small breasts, her navel, the hot carnivorous flower of her sex. I think somehow that my life would be complete forever if I could just have one chance to please her, if I could feel the muscles of her cunt seizing around my fingers, make her scream, feel her thighs shaking in my hands.

"Everything's ready to go," she says, pulling off her helmet and setting it on the worktable. Black tendrils of hair that have come loose from her messy bun trail down her chest and shoulders, touching her in ways that I wish I could. Blood rushes to my cheeks as I follow Dylan and Serje to the back table where she has our order stored in a haphazard pile of other projects—some artistic, some practical. Serje takes one of the climbing spurs in his hand, a metal structure equipped with nail-sharp spikes that fastens to the bottom of a shoe with broad leather straps. He nods appreciatively and passes it to Dylan, who tests the sharpness on his index finger and beams at Raph, throwing his arms around her.

"You saved us!" He laughs, exhaling the weight of months of stress and panic, and Raph gives me an aw-shucks kind of smirk over his shoulder. I feel my cheeks flush even hotter, my stomach roiling. Mia's apple moonshine is sitting badly with what little I managed to eat throughout the day, and I'm worried suddenly that I'll vomit from the nervousness.

"Hey, where's your bathroom?" I stammer, and Raph looks up from demonstrating the spurs to my enraptured friends. "It's the door that isn't my bedroom," she says, rifling through the pocket of her coveralls and handing me a lighter. "No light in the bathroom," she explains. "Just remember to blow the candles out when you're done."

I rush through the door, into the house's little kitchen, past the closed door of the room where Raph sleeps. The bathroom is tiny, not more more than a closet. When I light one of the candles mounted above the sink I see that its far wall is decorated in an odd mosaic of broken pieces of mirror and glass, different shades and textures of glass swirling together in wave-like patterns. The whole piece is bordered by a frame that looks like filigree made of scrap metal, motley pieces of copper and steel and brass weaving together like tangled tree roots.

I lean over the sink and splash cold water on my face, trying to get a decent look at myself in the bits of shattered glass, pulling my scraggly hair free from its braid and combing it with my fingers. I run my hands over my body, wishing I could see better how I look, eventually resolving to take off my baggy sweater and tie it around my waist, thinking maybe my white undershirt will be more presentable. The feeling of nausea washes over me again, and I sit down on the seat of the toilet and hold my head in my hands. It's been a long time since I slept for a full eight hours. I will my rational mind to overpower my emotions, telling myself we should head back as soon as possible so that the others are less vulnerable if anything happens. Caring about something larger than oneself requires sacrifice, and I can't allow myself to lose track of what's really important.

I grind the palms of my hands into my eyes and am standing up to go back to the others, when I hear a knock at the door.

"Meghan?" Raph's soft, velvet-suede voice through the crack of the door. "Are you okay?"

"I—yeah, yeah, I'm okay," I say, opening the door and stepping out to where she stands in the hall, stripped down to a sweat-damp white t-shirt now, her coveralls undone and hanging down from her hips. "Sorry, I guess the stress is just getting to me." I laugh. "We should probably be getting back to—"

"They left ten minutes ago," she cuts in, and I'm stuck standing there with my mouth open.

"Yeah, Serje told me you were sticking around?" she asks, and for a moment my nervousness is replaced by a murderous rage. Then I look at her expectant face, the way her big eyes are fixed on me. My gaze shifts down to my shoes and my lips split into a reluctant smile, thinking about how I need to hug him forever when I get back to the camp.

I meet her eyes again and start trying to formulate something clever to say, but she takes my hand and pulls me down the hall. "I was actually hoping that you'd stay," she says, ushering me through the door of her room.

My eyes can barely take in my surroundings before she puts her hands over them, catching me off guard. Bright canvasses decorate her walls, probably pieces other artists have traded her for her metalwork. Her bed dominates most of the space, its wrought-iron frame an intricate mass of metal coils, like something a fairytale witch would sleep in.

"Are you ready?" she asks. Words fail me, so I just nod, and she spins me around before moving her hands to my shoulders. In front of me is a tree, its trunk made from braided coils of scrap metal, its thin branches arching over my head, glittering with hammered copper leaves and mirror shards that dangle like stagnant drops of rain.

"This... is beautiful," I stammer. "Is it a commission?"

"No," she laughs, close to my ear. "I just made it for me. For you. You inspired me."

She wraps her arms around me from behind, enveloping me in her warmth. I bite my lips to try to stop myself from smiling, let myself lean back against her.

"What are you going to do with it?" I ask, taking in the span of the branches, too wide to fit through the door of the room.

"Keep it in here," she says, extricating herself from our embrace and reaching for one of the white paraffin candles that stand on her bedside table next to a pile of dog-eared books. I try not to stare at the way the loose tendrils of her hair brush against her face, the heaviness of her eyelids as she takes a lighter from her pocket and transfers its flame to the candle's wick.

"It's actually my new lighting system." She smirks, bending to retrieve a box of more candles from underneath the bed. She takes five of them, lighting them so that the flames make the dim room's shadows dance over her face. She hands all but one of them to me, and then secures the one she's kept into a flower-shaped holder on one of the branches above us. I follow suit, marvelling at the intricacy of the petalled holders anchored to the tree's metal branches.

She turns off the solar light in the ceiling, and the room falls into darkness except for the halo around the tree. The glow of the candles refracts off the metallic, mirrored leaves, dappling the room in silver, the way moonlight looks filtered through the forest's canopy.

I grab her hand and pull her close to me, her chest against my back again, and the two of us breathe in unison. I want to tell her a thousand things: that she's brilliant, that she's beautiful, but any compliment would feel contrived, insufficient to describe what she means to me.

"I want you," I say, and when she exhales into my hair, gripping my hips with her strong hands, I know that she understands I don't just want her body. She presses into me, undoing my pants with one hand and tugging them down so the rough fabric of her coveralls is against my bare skin. She's leaning on my shoulder to brace herself while she strokes my ass, moving in maddeningly slow circles till she gets to my pussy, dipping her fingertips inside me. I try to push back against her but she takes her hand away and wraps her arms around my stomach, her hands moving up to cup my breasts underneath my shirt and bra, her thumbs toying with my nipples.

"You're so wet for me already?" She laughs. "I hardly touched you. You think about me, don't you?" She murmurs in my ear, pressing her hips into mine and sliding her hand down the front of my pants again, cupping my throbbing pussy and moving her palm back and forth. I can feel my face flush with embarrassment. She's rolling my nipple between her finger and thumb, her breath hot on my neck when she takes my earlobe into her mouth. Light from the hanging pieces of mirror plays against her smooth skin, and I reach up to touch her face, cupping her cheek in my palm.

"Why don't you show me how you think about me?" she whispers, taking my chin and turning my face to hers. Our mouths come together and she moans a bit before pulling away from me, running the tip of her tongue over my open lips.

"Show me," she coaxes. My heart hits my ribs when I meet her eyes, and I stop myself short of blurting out that I would do anything for her. "Take all this off," she murmurs, tugging my pants down lower, pushing me onto the bed. I pull my shirt over my head and yank my jeans off the rest of the way, leaning back on my hands, looking at her as I open my legs. Her eyes stay on mine but I can see her chest moving faster, her nipples hard under the thin fabric of her shirt.

She's looking at me in a way nobody has before, and I feel beautiful under her gaze. Precious and uncommon. I lick my fingers and run them up and down my cleft, opening it for her, tracing the thin folds of my labia. Her lips are parted slightly, those heavy eyelids turning her eyes into two narrow slits. I slide two fingers inside myself and look up at her standing fully clothed above me, leaning with both hands on her cane.

"Fuck me. Please." I breathe, and she smiles at me with her sharp kitten teeth. I watch her strip her clothes off, her body somehow even more perfect than I'd imagined it. Faint stretch marks tiger-stripe her hips and the tops of her thighs, dark nipples tipping her small, conical breasts. A long centipede scar runs down her left leg: another part of her, beautiful like the rest. She eases herself onto the bed and takes the tips of my breasts into her mouth, sucking until I can't stop myself from moaning, my hips writhing desperately.

"Turn around," she says, pushing me onto my stomach, my face down in the pillows. She rubs my ass and slaps it hard, moaning in appreciation when I tilt my hips up.

She runs her tongue from my pussy to my ass, licking me there in a slow rhythm while her fingertips swirl at my clit. I come so hard my whole body shakes, tensing up and then relaxing. She lets me catch my breath for a second before sliding her fingers inside me, circling my spot, pushing me over the edge again and again until I'm convulsing, no longer in control of the sounds that are coming out of my mouth. She lies beside me and our lips connect, wet and sweet.

"Was that all right?" she asks, and I laugh at her question, shoving her shoulder so she falls on her back, the beautiful expanse of her body laid out before me while I nudge her legs apart and kneel between them.

"I guess that's a yes." She smiles. I leave a trail of kisses across her neck and chest, lapping at her nipples, feeling them harden against my lips. She breathes deeper and I kiss my way down her stomach, kneading her fleshy thighs with my hands. I lick the edges of her slit while her hands grasp at fistfuls of my hair. Her clit is so engorged I can almost see it throbbing, and I feel like I'm torturing myself as much as I am her. I slide my tongue over it and we both moan, her hands holding me fast by the reins of my hair. Her pussy is so wet I can ease three fingers into her, slickness clenching around my knuckles. I lick her harder, pushing the tip of my tongue under her clit hood where I can feel the electricity of her nerve endings forming a closed circuit with mine, the two of us moving as one organism. I squeeze my thighs together and come too when she climaxes, her back arched and bucking, waves of heat washing through my sensitive body. We lie with our limbs tangled together like tree roots, sweat cooling on our skin.

The sun is rising outside, staining the tree-lined horizon in a pale wash of pink. In the forest, late-blooming wildflowers will be opening their petals soon, turning their faces up toward the sun, their colors tempting wasps and honeybees to come and drink their nectar, coat their legs in sticky pollen, and fertilize other flowers, make them heavy with seeds by the time autumn comes.

New seeds will always find their way into the earth, I think to myself. In the cracks between paving stones, on the embankments beside highways. In the poisoned earth of abandoned industrial fields and the damp rot of their ancestors' cut-down stumps. I think of all those new green saplings, opening their leaves towards the sun, and I bury my face in my lover's thick hair as I fall asleep.

CONTRIBUTORS

Lillian Marguerite works in a STEM field in the rust belt and is rather French. She is saving up for her mad scientist hideout. This is her first erotica sale.

Renata Piper (Ph.D.) is a small, furry animal that writes. It loves science, fantasy, poetry, long walks on the beach, and poking dead things with a stick. The story "Making Love" is a tribute, in its way, to Edward Gorey's classic erotic novel *The Curious Sofa*.

Moxie Marcus is a Midwestern writer with an abundance of fantasies and a minimum of free time. While she may not be as tech savvy as her characters, she is at least as geeky as they are. She can sometimes be found running her tumblr, moxiemarcus.tumblr.com.

TS Porter is a tiny geek frequently mistaken for a collection of knobbly twigs wearing glasses. When not sleeping, they are usually found obsessively writing or baking sweet delicacies. TS' physical location and momentum varies, but home is always online. They can be found at ts-porter.tumblr.com.

Eric Del Carlo's work has appeared in numerous Circlet Press anthologies over the years. His most recent erotic novels are the postapocalyptic gunslinger tale *After the Hell* and the werewolf book *Flesh and Moonlight*. His mainstream science fiction has appeared in *Asimov's* and *Strange Horizons*, as well as a host of other publications. Check out *The Golden Gate Is Empty*, an urban fantasy novel cowritten with his father Vic Del Carlo. Find Eric on Facebook for comments or questions.

Kelly Rose Pflug-Black is an award-winning writer of fiction, poetry, and critical journalism. Her work has appeared before in places like *Strange Horizons*, the *Toronto Star*, the *Feminist Wire*, the *Huffington Post*, *Ideomancer Speculative Fiction*, *Stone Telling*, *Counterpunch*, and many others. She lives in Toronto, where she is currently working on her MA at York University and organizing events and programs for LGBTQ youth. This is her first published piece of erotic fiction, which she is pretty excited about.

Other titles you may enjoy from Circlet Press!

Jacked In: Transhumanist Erotica
edited by Gabrielle Harbowy
ISBN: 294-0-14814-395-6

Seven sexy science fiction stories explore and celebrate the eroticism that becomes possible when humans are augmented and enhanced through technology. Cybernetic implants, interfaces, prosthetics, nanotech... and sex. With stories by Sasha Payne, Cynthia Hamilton, Nobilis Reed, and Peter Tupper.

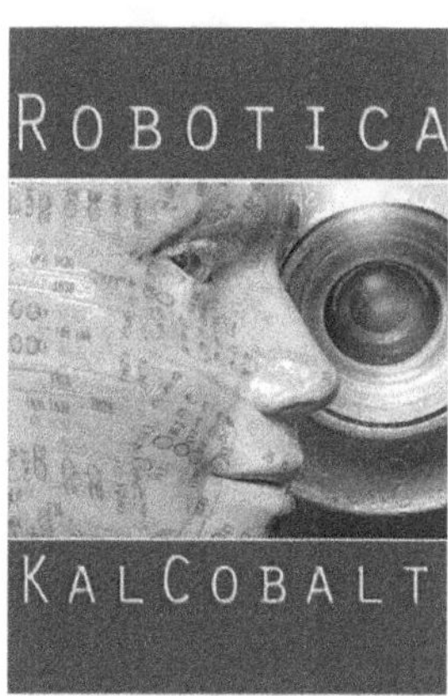

Robotica
by Kal Cobalt
ISBN: 294-0-04331-154-2

Five erotic stories of robot-human relations, exploring the future of humanity, sex, and desire. In Cobalt's futures, artificial intelligences can have very real emotions, and humans can be just as confused, turned on by, and obsessed with their robot lovers as they are by any others. The stories have a delicious homoerotic edge even as they question what gender means to a robot mind. Or heart.

Other titles you may enjoy from Circlet Press!

Simulacrum
by Rian Darcy
ISBN: 294-0-01478-226-5

In Simulnet, no one knows who you are: the perfect playground for the imagination... or a serial killer. The police ask Shaun to partner with an enigmatic programmer to hunt a murderer in the sex clubs and ramen shops of cyberspace. But as they investigate, Shaun finds himself wanting to know more about his partner. Ultimately the questions Shaun needs to answer are the ones deep in his heart.

Wired Hard 5
Edited by Joy Crelin
ISBN: 294-0-14853-379-5

This fifth volume in Circlet Press's Wired Hard anthology series collects five stories exploring gay male sexuality and themes of isolation and connection through the lens of erotic science fiction and fantasy. Wired Hard 5 includes stories by Jonathan Hepburn, Hero Freyr, Benji Bright, Laylah Hunter, and Sasha Payne.